DARK WITCH HELGA

LINDA C. LAND

Order this book online at www.trafford.com
or email orders@trafford.com

Most Trafford titles are also available at major online book retailers.

Printed in Victoria, BC, Canada.

ISBN: 978-1-4269-1868-1 (sc)

Library of Congress Control Number: 2009939483

*Our mission is to efficiently provide the world's finest, most comprehensive book publishing
service, enabling every author to experience success. To find out how to publish your
book, your way, and have it available worldwide, visit us online at www.trafford.com*

Trafford rev. 11/18/2009

www.trafford.com

North America & international
toll-free: 1 888 232 4444 (USA & Canada)
phone: 250 383 6864 ♦ fax: 812 355 4082

DEDICATION

This book is for Jordan and Lori. Your tender hearts, incredible creative talent, and superior intelligence provided the inspiration for the characters in this book.

To my daughter Michelle: Without your hours of editing and loads of great ideas this book would still be a rough manuscript lying on my desk. Thank you Michelle for taking the initiative to get this book published and most of all for believing in me.

Last but not least, thank you Beth for allowing us to get up close and personal with Sly.

PREFACE

When I was only five years old I walked to school every day. There was a very creepy old house at the bottom of our street. It was a basement house, and an elderly woman with hunched over posture lived there. I was an extremely friendly, talkative kid and spent many hours chatting with any of the neighbors who would listen to me, not that neighbor though! I let my overactive imagination get the better of me and dreamt of what might be going on in that scary house. That is how DARK WITcH HELGA was born.

CHAPTER ONE

Too Close To Helga

Helga was a witch. It was a secret that Jordan carried with her every day of her life. It was a terrible thing to have this knowledge and to keep it a secret. For Jordan, only 10 years old, it was the hardest thing she had ever had to do.

Jordan so badly wanted someone to talk to about Helga. How much longer could she keep quiet? 'Perhaps the whole neighborhood is in danger. Helga may be planning something terrible at this very minute.' And after what happened last night, she was desperate to talk to someone. What could she do? What should she do?' "Oh my," Jordan sighed out loud. "What am I going to do?"

The telephone rang, causing her to jump. She hopped out of bed and ran toward the kitchen. She could hear her mom talking to someone on the phone. Jordan heard her mom say, "Sure, that would be great. We would really like for Lori to stay with us for two weeks. Jordan would love it. She's been moping around the house too much lately." Hearing Jordan walk into the kitchen, her mom turned and winked at her as she finished her phone conversation with Aunt Di.

Jordan's whole face brightened with the news of her cousin's visit. It was as if her wish had been granted. She would tell Lori everything. She knew she could trust her with her secret, and Lori would know what to do.

By the time her mom hung up the phone Jordan was jumping up and down with excitement. She wanted to know everything. "When is Lori coming mom? Can she sleep in my bedroom with me every night? Can we stay up late and watch movies? Is Patty coming too?" Jordan shot one question after another, not giving her mother a chance to answer one before another spilled out of her mouth.

"Slow down Jordan," her mom said. "I knew this would cheer you up. Lori will be here Saturday. Aunt Di and Uncle Keith have to go out of town on business. And yes, of course she can sleep in your room with you, but I'm not so sure about watching movies until late at night. We'll have to talk to your dad about that. Patty is not coming with her. She is going to be at camp, so it's just you and Lori for two whole weeks. Now you'd better start thinking about getting your room straightened up. You have two days." Her mom patted her on the back and gave a big smile as she watched Jordan dance down the hallway to her room.

Jordan and Lori were only sixteen months apart in age. In early August Lori had turned twelve, and Jordan had turned ten back in April. There were a total of nine cousins on her mother's side of the family; seven girls and two boys. Lori had an older sister, Patty, who was fifteen and Jordan had a four year old little brother named Josh. Jordan enjoyed family holidays with all her cousins, but she especially enjoyed seeing Lori. There was an automatic connection between the two girls and there had been since they were very little. They just always seemed to understand each other.

Jordan was extremely excited about Lori staying for two weeks.

2

She would have someone to talk to other than Josh. Josh could be a lot of fun, but Jordan needed someone she could confide in, and her little brother was definitely not what she needed right now. Jordan had to share her worries with someone her age, someone who would understand and maybe have some ideas of what she should do.

Helga…Helga is the name that Jordan had given the old lady that lived just five houses down the street. No one in the neighborhood knew the woman's real name. In fact, no one knew much of anything about her. Helga was more than just strange, or odd. She was weird. Her house was spooky and even her yard was ugly. The old lady lived in what Jordan's dad called a basement house. It was a basement that never had a house built on top of it. It was just a flat, dark ugly square with short, cold gray walls. There was only one small window and a short, square front door. The house could not be seen in the summer due to all the trees, tall grasses, and weeds that filled the yard. The old woman's house could be seen more clearly in the winter time, but even then no one really wanted to look at it because it was so ugly.

The neighborhood where Jordan lived was an older neighborhood. All of the houses had been built nearly 100 years ago. The homes were brick with big front porches that stretched across the entire front of the house. Many of them, including Jordan's house, had dusty attics and cool stone basements. All the neighbors took excellent care of their houses and yards, all except Helga. Her nasty yard and old basement house just didn't fit, and neither did Helga. The neighbors were friendly and enjoyed visiting with each other, all except Helga. Everyone knew everyone else's business, and sometimes knew more than you wanted them to know, but not Helga. No one seemed to know much of anything about her. Even the neighbors that had lived there for years knew little about her. All they knew was that she had lived there longer than anyone else had, and that she lived alone. No one had ever seen her go farther than her own yard. The thing that really gave Jordan the creeps though, was that no one had ever seen her face.

Helga was a mystery, and a spooky one at that. Jordan remembered one particular night when her family was driving down the street toward home. Her curiosity found her staring out the window as they passed Helga's house. She'll never forget what she saw. Strange colors glowed through the tiny window. Colored smoke oozed out of the chimney. Goosebumps ran up her arm even now, remembering that night. Weird! Everything about the house and the old woman was just plain weird. Helga didn't fit. She was nothing like the other people in the neighborhood and she was nothing like Jordan.

Jordan had sun streaked blond hair and curious blue-green eyes. She was always full of intelligent questions about everything and everyone, and she loved being in the middle of every conversation. Jordan was a friendly kid. She was innocent and kind and had always been quick to warm up to strangers. Unfortunately, that changed about five years ago when she first started school. That was the first time she found herself up close to Helga.

It was August and Jordan was five years old; ready and eager to start school. She had been looking so forward to all the new exciting things that awaited her. She was eager to meet new people and make friends with kids her own age. She knew she would love everything about going to school.

Her school was only six blocks from her house, and because of that she would not be riding the bus. Instead, she would walk to school every day. To Jordan, this sounded like great fun. It gave her a sense of freedom and made her feel grown up. The first couple weeks her mom drove her to school every day, and picked her up each afternoon when school got out. Each day in the car her mom would tell her that soon she would have to walk to school all by herself. Jordan wasn't the least bit afraid or worried about it. Her mom cautioned her about several things that all moms worry about. She said, "Jordan, you must be very careful and always come straight home every day. Don't talk to strangers, or ever get in the car with anyone other than me or daddy." Her mom would say the same thing every day she drove her to school until Jordan had every word memorized. It frightened her a little because she could hear the concern in her mother's voice. Jordan wondered why her mom sounded that way.

After the first two weeks of being driven to school, her mom spent the next few weeks walking with her to school. Jordan didn't think this was at all necessary and couldn't wait until the day she would be on her own.

That first morning they walked together to school was beautiful and sunny. Jordan was very happy. Even though she wasn't walking all by herself, it was still thrilling. She couldn't wait until the morning she would walk all by herself. Jordan was delighted that she would never have to wait on a bus to pick her up every morning, and she could always head for home the minute school was out each afternoon.

As they walked, her mom was running through the same rules as she had done for the last two weeks in the car. "Remember to always come straight home." Jordan wasn't really listening. She had heard it all so many times. Instead, she tilted her head back just a little and let the warm sun hit her face. She skipped along, lost in her own thoughts. She hummed a tune as she bounced along....until they came to the 5th house down the street. The old basement house.

Suddenly, everything around her seemed to change. It smelled and felt damp. The sun seemed to disappear, and Jordan could feel the darkness close in around her. All her cheery thoughts began to fade away. Unconsciously, she moved closer to her mother's side. Her blue-green eyes widened as she looked around with curious attention. Jordan squinted her eyes to see the cave-like house that was hidden in the tall weeds. As she focused on the nasty yard, something caught her attention. What was it? She wasn't sure. She could feel knots pull in her stomach, like the ones she got when she was car sick. She blinked her eyes, and then rubbed them with her fist. She stared back into the darkness of the yard, blinking her eyes again to focus them.

For a frightening moment she thought she saw a pair of eyes staring back at her; strange, large, yellow eyes. Now if that didn't frighten her enough, the next thing that happened surely did. Her mother gently wrapped her arm around Jordan protectively, and without a word guided her across to the other side of the street. Jordan looked back toward the yard. It was gone. Whatever she thought she saw was gone. Maybe it was never there. Maybe it was only her imagination. The rest of their journey to school was spent in silence. Thousands of unspoken questions raced through Jordan's head; questions laced with curiosity and fear.

That afternoon when school was out, her mom was waiting there for her. They walked home in pleasant conversation, until they once again came to the weird house at the bottom of their street. Jordan felt her mother's arm wrap around her shoulders, and she once again guided them to the far side of the street, away from Helga's house. Jordan wanted to ask her mother why this old house felt so creepy, but she knew it was something her mom would not talk about so she decided not to bring it up.

The routine continued with her mom walking with her to and from school for the next two weeks. Her mom wanted to be sure that Jordan knew the way, and that she remembered everything she had told her to do, and *not* to do. By the time Jordan walked to school by herself for the first time, she was both excited and frightened. She left the house that morning with pure determination. She was grown up now and she could do this all by herself. As she approached the bottom of the street and came upon the ugly old basement house, she squinted her eyes nearly shut and crossed over to the other side of the street just as her mom had done. She was so proud of herself once she was well out of sight of Helga's house. A big smile covered her face. "I did it," she said to herself. That wasn't so bad, she thought. She bounced with glee and skipped off to school. Each day became easier and her confidence grew, until Jordan didn't even notice the old house at the bottom of the street. Every day when she approached Helga's house she crossed over to the far side of the street, not even looking over at the spooky old place. She was so proud of herself, and she wondered what she had been so afraid of. It was just an ugly old house with an unfriendly old woman living in it; that was all. Everything was going to be just fine. But then, it happened.

It was her second week of walking alone, and she was on her way home. As Jordan thought back to that day her memories were as clear as if it had all just happened. It was a lovely fall day, with the sun pouring down its warmth through the clear blue afternoon sky. The colorful fall leaves were already littering the ground along the streets and sidewalks. Jordan was just a few houses away from home, listening to the sound her shoes made as they crunched over the crisp leaves. She noticed two little squirrels playing in the street right in front of her. One of them had a big nut in its mouth and the other one was chasing him around in circles.

"Humph," Jordan said aloud. "Hey little guy, is he trying to take your nut from you? Maybe he should go find his own and leave you alone!" She spoke in a soft and friendly voice, not wanting to scare them away. To her total surprise, both squirrels stopped and sat up on their back legs as she spoke, looking straight at her. It was as if they heard her and understood what she was saying to them. Jordan's eyes grew as big as saucers. She let out a little giggle, and decided to see just how close she could get to them.

She took just a few small steps so as not to alarm them. She inched her way closer. When she was only a short distance from them they sprang into action and bounced a short distance from her. Jordan stopped immediately and froze. She didn't want them to run off, and she was pleased to see that they had stopped and were still very close to her. Again they sat up on their back legs and looked back at her. She was so surprised at their friendly behavior. Jordan was a very smart five-year old. She knew this was very unusual behavior for squirrels, but they were so cute. Again, she inched her way toward them, and again they moved away just far enough to stay out of her reach. "You're teasing me, aren't you?" she whispered. "You're not going to let me get close enough to pet you, are you?"

Jordan wasn't ready to give up. Letting out a giggle, she moved toward them. Reaching out her open hand she tried to encourage them to trust her, but they spun around and jumped off the road into some tall grass. Jordan thought they were gone, but she was tickled to see they had stopped and were looking back at her. It was a funny sight to see their tiny bodies stretched up as tall as they could, peeking over the top of the grass.

To Jordan it was about the cutest thing she had ever seen and she bounced right off the road and into the tall grass after them. All her attention was totally focused on the two funny little squirrels. She saw the squirrels jump into a small bush. "So, now you want to play hide and seek," Jordan said through giggles. "Okay, here I come!" Jordan bent over the bush in search of the frisky duo. As she started to part the branches, she heard music. She straightened up and took a couple steps backward. 'That was strange,' she thought to herself. 'How could there be music coming out of a bush?' Jordan's curiosity got the best of her and she slowly moved forward toward the bush.

She bent down and listened, trying to determine if indeed the music was coming from the bush, or from somewhere else. The tiny delicate sound was beautiful. Slowly, she pulled the branches apart and revealed a beautiful music box sitting on a tree stump behind the bush. It was made of gold and crystal. The sunlight hit the crystals, making the box shine with many vibrant colors. For a moment she felt herself lost in the lovely music coming from the music box. It was soft and gentle. Then she heard a rustling sound. 'It must be the squirrels I almost forgot about.' She pulled her attention from the music box in search of the furry little friends she had made.

To her dismay, it was not the squirrels that she saw looking back at her. Instead, two large glowing eyes stared directly at her. She jumped back and fell to the ground. She fell so hard that she hit the back of her head. Her eyes shut tight with the pain. She quickly sat up and rubbed the back of her head, afraid to open her eyes. She did not want to look up and see those yellow eyes staring back at her. Then she heard a strange noise. Slowly, she forced her eyes open and looked up from the grass that surrounded her. Jordan's eyes locked onto a sight nothing could have prepared her for. Standing right in front of her was an old woman. Stunned and unable to move, Jordan just stared up at her in horror. The woman was dressed in a long black rag of a dress that hung on her shapeless body. A black hood covered her head. Her back slumped over in an awkward position as if it were broken. Her long gray hair hung over her face, totally hiding it from Jordan's view. Looming there above Jordan, the woman's claw-like hand reached out toward her.

That was all it took to break Jordan from her shocked trance. She jumped to her feet and ran across the yard as fast as she could, stumbling all the way through the weeds and brush until at last she was on the smooth hard surface of the road. Out of nowhere, the loud honking of a car horn filled her ears. A car rushed toward her. A new kind of terror suddenly gripped her heart. She froze, unable to force her feet to move. Then something truly amazing happened.

She felt two strong arms lift her and move her body from the road to the grassy edge as the car sped past her and out of sight. She looked all around, but saw no one. Jordan was in shock. Her shaky legs and weak knees forced her to collapse to the ground. What had just happened? Who pulled her out of the way of that car? Once she calmed down some, she picked herself up off the ground. She had the feeling someone was watching her. As she glanced back toward the old woman's yard, she caught sight of those same yellow eyes. Directly above the eyes she thought she could make out the shape of two huge black pointed things. Fear gripped her by the throat again and she ran for home, forcing herself not to look back.

She ran straight through the front door of her house, down the hall, and into her room, slamming her bedroom door shut behind her. She threw herself on her bed. She really wanted to run to her mother's arms, but was afraid her mother would be angry and disappointed in her for not coming straight home as she had taught her to do. And if her mom knew she had run out in the street without looking both ways first…well…Jordan knew her mom would never let her walk to school alone again. She would have to keep this a secret.

She didn't sleep at all that first night. She kept replaying the entire incident over and over in her mind. She was convinced the woman who lived in the basement house was a witch. That's when she gave her a name…Helga. She knew now that the two black pointed things she saw must have been the large ears of a very big dog or maybe even a wolf, and those yellow eyes belonged to the same creature. She was also sure that those were the same pair of eyes that were in the bushes, and the same ones she saw staring at her that first day her mother walked her to school. Shaking, she buried her head under her pillow trying to block out the fear that surrounded her. She could have been killed by that car. Who had saved her?

She shook her head in an effort to clear her mind of the memories of that scary day, years ago. Her thoughts and fears of Helga had not kept her from bravely walking back and forth to school every day since then. She crossed to the other side of the road each day, just as her mom had taught her, and she was careful not to get too distracted by playful squirrels. Most days, she didn't even let her eyes wander over toward Helga's yard. But after last night, she wasn't sure she would ever be able to walk past that house again.

CHAPTER 2

Lori's Visit

Jordan jumped when she heard her mom's voice calling to her. Jordan was a sound sleeper, but lately her nights had been filled with strange dreams. The spooky dreams about Helga had become a nightly terror for her. She hadn't had a good night's sleep in a very long time. The dreams were always similar, Helga reaching out for her, pleading for Jordan's help. And then she would find herself in a dark place. It looked like a long, dark tunnel and she heard a strange humming sound. It just didn't make any sense, but dreams never make sense. She just wanted them to stop. Last night was different though. She wasn't so sure last night's dream was a dream. In fact, she was certain it was real.

She was asleep, dreaming the same strange dreams, until the soft gentle sound of music pulled her awake. It filled her room. For a moment, she couldn't tell if she was still sleeping or if she was awake. She looked around, trying to figure out where the music was coming from. She was scared, and her body felt cold.

She again had the sense that someone was watching her. As she looked toward her window, she spotted two large, yellow eyes staring in at her from outside. The memories of that scary day years earlier came rushing back into her mind and she recognized the tune of the music that filled her ears. It was the same as the music box from Helga's yard. As she stared out her window, she could barely make out the silhouette of large ears. A small circle of fog appeared on her window from the hot breath of the beast. Quickly, she thrust the bed covers up over her head. Instantly, the music stopped and her room was still. She peeked out from beneath the covers. The yellow eyes were gone. She watched the circle of fog fade away. There would be no restful sleep for Jordan tonight.

When she got up that morning she couldn't stop staring out the window. She couldn't wait to talk to Lori. The secret she had kept for so long would finally be shared. Her mom called out again. Breakfast was ready. As she ate, they discussed their plans for the day and the preparations needed for Lori's visit. She busied herself and tried to forget about her worries. Lori would be there in two days, and everything would be better then.

The next day flew by. Her mom had several errands to run. After that Jordan spent the rest of the day playing with her little brother. She had her room all clean and ready for her cousin's arrival the next day.

That night, Jordan had a hard time getting to sleep. She was so excited about Lori's visit. She had so many things she wanted to tell her, but as she went over it all in her mind, it sounded really crazy. 'Will Lori believe me? How much should I tell her, and what part should I not tell?' she wondered. She thought about how she would explain it. Maybe she shouldn't tell her about what happened that day five years ago; the day she followed the squirrels into Helga's yard. It had been so long ago; maybe it would be best to skip that part. Yes, that would be better. Finally Jordan fell asleep, but her dreams haunted her all night.

The next morning Jordan drug herself out of bed. She was

moving slow, but eager for the day to begin. She got dressed and went to the kitchen to find her mom. Josh wasn't up yet, so her mom sat down with her at the table while she ate a quick bowl of cereal.

"Well, I expected you to be bouncing off the walls this morning. Lori will be here any time now," her mom said, looking at her with concern on her face.

"Oh, I am happy, very happy. I'm just not awake yet, that's all."

Just then Josh popped around the corner with a morning grin on his face and jumped into a chair.

"That's more like it," her mom said, looking at Josh and ruffling his hair.

Josh let a big smile cover his happy face. Mom got up from the table and busied herself fixing his breakfast. Jordan sat there for awhile talking to her mom and her brother.

"So," her mom asked, "What do you have planned for your first day with Lori?"

Jordan looked up in surprise. She hadn't thought of anything except sharing her darkest fears. Stuttering just a bit Jordan replied, "I-I-thought we could read that new book my friend gave me." Not knowing what else to say and not wanting to say the wrong thing, Jordan excused herself to go to her room and make her bed. She said she wanted everything just right by the time Lori arrived.

When the door bell rang, Jordan ran from her room. Dashing down the hall she beat her brother to the front door. Her mom was right behind them and greeted Aunt Di and Lori with a warm hug. Jordan and Lori went out to the car to carry in Lori's suitcases and backpack and several other items Lori had brought for her two week stay. Lori was like any other female, she packed heavy. Once they had everything in Jordan's room it was time for Lori to tell her mom goodbye. Her mom told her she would call and check on her every day or so, and warned her to be good, which wasn't necessary. Lori was always good and never any trouble. She gave Lori a big squeeze of a hug, and out the door she went. Everyone waved goodbye.

Jordan's mom turned to them and said, "You kids go find something to do while I clean up the kitchen. Later I might pack a picnic lunch and you can all eat outside. Would you like that?"

Three big smiles looked up at her, and her mom knew they loved the idea. "Yeah," Jordan beamed, "That would be fun. Thanks mom." All three kids ran back to Jordan's room.

"Well," Jordan said, "What do you want to do first?" Before Lori could reply, Josh spoke up. "Let's go outside and play hide and seek," he said, jumping up and down with excitement. Josh had been just as eager for Lori's visit as Jordan had been. Jordan had already been warned by her mom that she couldn't leave her brother out of everything. She would have to include him at least part of the time.

Lori was a very easy going kind of kid, with big blue eyes and warm brown hair. Lori looked at Josh. Smiling down at him she quickly agreed. "Sure, that sounds like fun," Lori said. They all left the bedroom and headed down the hall, through the kitchen, and out the back door.

Jordan and Lori walked side by side as Josh led the way. Jordan was so happy that her cousin was finally there, she didn't care what they did. She knew that she wouldn't have a chance to really talk to Lori until that night. She realized she would have to be very careful not to talk about Helga around Josh, because he might tell her mom and that would not be good.

They played outside all morning and stopped only long enough to eat the lunch Jordan's mom had brought out to them. They spread an old blanket under the biggest tree in the yard. Josh had brought out his crazy eight cards and they played while they ate. It was so much fun. Jordan pushed all her worries aside. It was the first time in weeks that Helga had not filled her mind. It was a wonderful day.

CHAPTER 3

Shared Secrets

After dinner that evening the girls helped Jordan's mom clean up the kitchen. Jordan's mom took Josh to get him cleaned up for bed and the girls went to Jordan's room. They were both tired after playing outside all day.

As they started getting ready for bed Lori told Jordan all about a book she had just finished reading. "It was a mystery and was the spookiest book I have ever read. I loved it." Lori pulled back the covers. "I can't wait 'til my mom takes me to the library again. I am going to try to find another book by the same author. I think I love mysteries. The story was about a young girl who had become a detective. The book told of many adventures and near tragedies the main character experienced. I think it would be awesome to do some of the incredible things the character in the book did."

Jordan thought this was the perfect moment to bring up her problem. Now was the time to tell Lori all about Helga. Taking a big breath, she slowly climbed into bed and turned out the bedside light. "Lori, if you love mysteries, how would you like to help me solve a *real* mystery? I have a problem, a big problem, and I want your help with it. It's something that's been bothering me for a long time, but I've been too afraid to tell anyone."

"What is it Jordan, what's wrong?" Lori asked, with deep concern in her voice.

"Well, it's going to be hard to believe. That's why I haven't told anyone. I'm afraid no one will believe me."

"I'll believe you, I promise," Lori said. She was very interested and a bit excited to hear about Jordan's mystery.

Those were the words Jordan needed to hear. She sat up in bed and reached over for the bedside lamp. She clicked it on and spun around to face Lori. "You promise, you really promise?"

Lori sat up and smiled at Jordan. "Of course I will." She turned around and propped up her pillow, as if getting ready to hear a good bedtime story. She got comfortable and motioned for her cousin to do the same, but Jordan was too excited.

She gazed into her cousin's face. Lori could sense the seriousness of the situation. "Lori, there is a witch living down the street. She is weird and she is evil, and I'm worried about what she is up to." Without stopping, Jordan continued explaining the strange colors she has seen coming from the old lady's chimney late at night. And about how no one in the neighborhood seemed to know anything about her. She did not tell her about the dreams, her first encounter with Helga, or the eyes she saw through her window just a few days before. Not yet.

"Lori, I need your help. I wish I could get my parents to move before Helga does something to hurt us, but what about everyone else in the neighborhood? I can't turn my back on them. I want to know what Helga is up to.

Jordan fell back into her pillow as if exhausted. She squeezed her eyes shut and held her breath, waiting for her cousin's response. She was so worried that Lori would brush off her fears, or even worse, not believe her. But to Jordan's pure joy, Lori did just the opposite.

"Jordan, this Helga sounds very strange. Even her name is spooky," Lori said, deep in thought.

"Well, I don't know what her real name is, that's the name I gave her. I had to call her something, so I decided Helga fit. I asked everyone in the neighborhood about her, but not one has ever spoken to her, no one." Jordan looked down and nervously fidgeted with the blankets, feeling both relieved and scared.

Lori reached over and patted Jordan on the hand. "What do you want to do?"

Jordan looked up at Lori. Her eyes filled with tears. "I don't know what to do, and that's why I need your help. How can we prove to everyone that Helga is a witch? And most important, how can we stop her from doing something awful?"

Lori's eyes were filled with interest and empathy. She didn't believe in witches, but she did believe in bad people. She knew that sometimes people could be cruel and even dangerous. She didn't want to hurt her cousin's feelings by telling her there was no such thing as witches. However, she did believe that something wasn't right about this old woman Jordan called Helga. She wanted to get a look at the house, and Helga's yard for herself. And if she was lucky, she would like to get a peek at Helga. To Lori, this was a chance to do something heroic, something mysterious. "What do you think she's up to?" Lori asked, wanting more details.

"I'm not sure, but during the last week of school I heard some very weird noises, and smelled something strange every time I passed by her house. Something like I have never smelled before. I am so afraid that she is up to something very bad." Jordan had told Lori everything she could think of regarding the house, and the yard, and Helga…almost everything. She knew no one would believe the awful vision of Helga and she didn't want to tell Lori about the eyes, she just didn't. But, should she mention the dreams?

"Lori, there is something else. I have been having a lot of dreams, always the same, but they don't make any sense." Jordan told Lori about her dreams, and Lori thought they were very interesting.

"Well," Lori said, "I need to get a look at this place. I have an idea." Lori lowered her voice. Glancing over at the clock on Jordan's bedside table she noted the time. It was 9:30. "Jordan, let's go down to Helga's house. I want to see it. Maybe we'll even see the smoke you talked about."

Jordan sat up very tall, as if her back was stiff as a board. She backed away from her cousin a little and opened her mouth to speak, but no words would come out. She blinked her eyes and cleared her throat. "Lori, I have only seen the smoke a couple of times from our car when we drove by her house after dark. I don't think you will be able to see it. How are we going to get my mom to take us someplace now? It's so late, and we're already in bed? I mean we can't, you don't….?" Jordan's voice trailed off. She swallowed hard, looking over at her cousin. Jordan realized what Lori really wanted to do. "Lori, you mean now, right now, I can't, we can't."

"Jordan, it's okay. We just go out the back door and walk down the street and have a peek. It won't take us 10 minutes. Then we'll come right back, I promise." Lori was not the kind of kid to sneak out of her own house at night, not to mention sneak out of her cousin's house, but her curiosity had completely taken over. Jordan felt Lori tug on her hand and felt her feet slip out from under the covers and touch the floor. Lori pulled her along. Both girls slipped on their robes and slippers. Lori opened Jordan's door just a crack. The house was quiet and mostly dark. There was a soft light coming from down the hall. Jordan's mom and dad were either watching TV or working on the computer, and their door was closed. The coast was clear. Lori motioned to Jordan, and out the door and down the hall they tip-toed. Lori was very careful not to let the back door make any noise as they left the house.

Once outside the safety of her house, Jordan almost panicked. She grabbed Lori by the shoulder and started shaking her. "Lori, we can't do this. We have to go back inside. What if something happens to us? What if Helga sees us?"

"Jordan, it will be okay. We will stay out of sight, no one will see us. Just stay close to me."

"No problem," Jordan said under her breath. "You couldn't get me further than one inch from you! No problem!" Jordan shook her head back and forth as they crept around the house and headed for the street. She couldn't believe she was doing this. She must be crazy. Why was she allowing Lori to talk her into doing something like this? She knew why. It was because Lori believed her. Lori wanted to do something about Helga, and that's what Jordan wanted too. She just hadn't expected Lori to act so quickly, or so boldly. She certainly hadn't expected Lori to want to go out in the dark to the spookiest place on earth... Helga's house...in the dark.

Jordan could feel the butterflies in her tummy jumping with excitement and fear. The kind of fear that gives you goose bumps all over, even on your face and the back of your neck. It felt like tiny bugs crawling all over her skin. She was so lost in her feelings that when Lori reached out and touched her arm, Jordan jumped and let out an air cracking scream...aww!

Lori was more than a little surprised by her cousin's reaction. She immediately apologized. "Oh my, I'm sorry Jordan. I didn't mean to frighten you. Don't be so jumpy. There is nothing to worry about, you'll see."

Jordan didn't respond. She just nodded her head quietly and tried to calm herself by gulping in big breaths of fresh air. She couldn't make Lori understand the seriousness of the situation. There were so many things to worry about, not to mention the fact that they had snuck out of the house without telling her mom. Jordan had never done anything like that before. Jordan's worried thoughts were pushed aside as her cousin's soft voice floated across the still night air.

"Jordan, is this the place?" Lori pointed a finger toward the wide space of trees and tall grass directly in front of them. She felt Jordan's hand reach out to hold hers. She knew by the tight squeeze Jordan had on her that this was the place where the old lady lived. Lori walked closer, pulling Jordan along. She was on her tip-toes, trying her best to see over the weeds. Then it happened. Lori saw something that made her blood run cold. Two enormous yellow eyes. They looked at her so deeply that she could feel her heart jumping in her chest. She quickly blinked her eyes and stepped backward. Then they were gone. She shook her head to clear the vision, to remove the bright spots that remained. Blinking, she scanned the weeds, but didn't see the creepy yellow globes anywhere.

Still holding tightly to Lori's hand Jordan noticed her cousin tense up and step backward. In a tight high voice Jordan whispered, "What's wrong, what do you see?" Lori didn't say anything, but even in the dark Jordan could see her cousin shake her head back and forth. Whatever it was now wasn't the time to talk about it, Jordan thought.

The night air moved with a cold heaviness that held danger within it. The shadowy light from the full moon overhead only added to the eerie atmosphere. It was a feeling that caused Lori to shiver. The breeze was strong enough to sway the tree limbs and the brush enough to give Lori a short but clear view of the basement house. Lori stepped back again. She didn't want to speak her thoughts out loud. Jordan was already frightened, and she knew if she said what she was thinking Jordan would bolt for home. Keeping her voice calm she answered, "This place is strange. I've never seen anything like it before." She paused. "Don't you think that's why it's so scary to you, because it's so different?" Lori didn't know what else to say.

Jordan wanted to go. As she tugged on her cousin's hand she whispered, "Come on Lori. This place is creepy enough in the daytime, I want to go home."

Silently, Lori nodded her head up and down in agreement. As Lori allowed Jordan to pull her away, she got a glimpse of something. It was those two yellow things, eyes. They were eyes looking at her from the tall grass, following her every step. Lori squeezed her eyes shut and turned her head away.

Still holding hands the girls slowly walked up the street. Both remained silent. Both were deep in their own thoughts.

Lori wanted to keep the vision of the weird eyes to herself for now. 'Gosh,' Lori thought, 'if the house is this spooky from the outside, what would the inside be like, and what did those eyes belong to?' Lori felt a shiver run down her back.

Lori's whisper finally broke the silence. Lori tried to sound mildly curious instead of fearful. "Jordan, have you ever seen Helga, I mean ever?"

Jordan sensed Lori was holding something back, as if she wanted to say more but stopped short. Lori's question brought back the vision of Helga. Jordan's mind filled with the dark image. Helga's stooped shoulders and bent back, the long strings of gray hair swirling around her dark black hood which she kept pulled over her head, and the claw like hand. Jordan's head nodded up and down slowly at first and then faster, until her hair was whipping her in the face. Jordan stopped walking. Taking a deep breath she looked over at her cousin. Softly, she let the words slip from her lips. "Yes, I did. I am the only one in the neighborhood who has ever seen her face to face, sort of. I'm sorry I didn't tell you earlier." Jordan let go of Lori's hand and folded her arms across her chest, letting her gaze fall to the ground.

Lori's eyes grew huge in the darkness. "What did she look like? Have you ever seen the inside of her house?"

Jordan's head snapped up. "Lori, are you out of your mind? I won't even step in to her yard, not ever again, much less in to that black hole she uses as a house!"

"You have been in her yard before, and you didn't tell me that either! How close were you to her, and did you see the eyes?" Lori couldn't hold back any longer. She was full of questions. She wanted to know every bit of information her cousin knew about this place.

At first Jordan was shocked that Lori mentioned the eyes, but then she thought about it. Lori must have seen them. They were real. She wasn't sure why that should make her feel better, but it did. "You saw the eyes, the big yellow eyes?" Jordan got the answer she wanted by the sudden look on Lori's face, and the sharp surprised breath her cousin drew in.

"Yes I did, and by the sound of your voice you have too. What about Helga? You haven't told me everything about Helga, have you Jordan?"

Jordan felt a little uneasy. There was that one time she *had* been up close to Helga, but she couldn't see her face. The dark hood and long tangled gray hair cancelled her face from view. The other times she had seen her were always from a distance, and Helga always had her back to her. "Lori, no one has seen Helga's face. Not even me, and I was as close to her as I am you right now."

"What did you see, if not her face?"

Jordan placed her hands on her hips. "Her face was covered by her long gray hair, and hidden back inside the black hood she always wears over her head. All the other times have been from the road, always, but I can tell you that I saw enough to know she's a witch!" Jordan described the day that she followed the squirrels into Helga's yard, and that she had seen the big yellow eyes too, but she wasn't completely sure until now if they were real or just her imagination. Jordan's voice grew louder, "She is a witch I tell you, *she is!*"

Lori reached over and patted Jordan's shoulder. "It's okay Jordan, everything is okay. I agree with you," she replied, wanting to reassure her cousin that she was on her side. "There is something very odd about Helga." Lori left her words floating in the air, keeping the rest of her thoughts to herself. She just didn't believe in witches, and she wondered if maybe Jordan was stretching her memory of that day just a little. After all, that was five years ago, and she was only five years old at the time. She knew her cousin was telling her the truth as she remembered it.

Either way, if this old woman keeps her face hidden and looks like Jordan said, then there was something very spooky going on. Why would anyone do that?

"What about the eyes, what do you think they are?" Jordan asked her cousin. "I'll tell you what I think they are. I think they belong to Helga's pet. Most witches have a black cat, but I think Helga has a black wolf!"

Lori faced Jordan in the darkness. She didn't know what to say. "I don't know what they belong to Jordan, I only know they were creepy."

Both girls started walking toward home. It was late and the middle of the dark road was not the best place to have a witch debate. Lori had a lot of things to try to figure out. She couldn't get the image of those yellow eyes out of her head. They were so bright. Even for the short second she saw them they left her blinking her eyes and seeing spots, like when someone takes your picture and the flash causes you to see bright spots. Lori had to shake her head to clear her mind. She just realized her cousin had been jabbering the whole time about Helga. Lori pretended she had heard everything Jordan had been saying, but what *was* she saying? Something about Helga being a witch. Lori tried to jump into the conversation. "Jordan, I'm not so sure I believe in witches."

Jordan stopped in her tracks. "Lori, what's the matter with you?" Jordan strained her eyes to see her cousin's face in the darkness. "You act as if you haven't listened to anything I've told you."

Lori shuddered, shaking off any remaining thoughts of the piercing eyes from her memory. She wondered if they were Helga's eyes. 'No way,' she thought.

When Lori remained silent Jordan became agitated. "You think I'm being silly. You don't believe anything I've said. Even after seeing that cave she calls a house, and the weird eyes," her voice cracked and her hands flew around in the air. She was just about to burst into tears, when Lori turned to face her trembling, younger cousin. She took both her hands and gently put them on Jordan's shoulders. She looked Jordan square in the face. "I'm sorry Jordan. I don't know what to say, except you're right. I think you're right about everything. Really, I do!"

Jordan's eyes glistened with unshed tears. A slow smile covered her face as her cousin's words sunk in. Jordan threw her arms around Lori's neck and she jumped up and down. "You do, you do…you believe me? You think Helga's a witch too!"

Lori allowed Jordan this moment of joy. She didn't want to spoil it. She waited a few minutes, and then she chose her words very carefully. "Jordan, whether Helga is a witch or a really awful person, or maybe just strange looking, we need to get a closer look at her and her house. We need to figure it out. If she's a bad person, we need to tell someone before something awful happens, but we need proof. Otherwise no one will do anything about it.

Jordan's smile began to fade. "Lori, what do you mean we need to get a closer look? You saw that place tonight. You even stepped back after just one small glance at it. And if she is a witch…or a bad person…or whatever…how can we find out anything? We could end up as her dinner. That's what witches do to kids you know!"

Lori interrupted Jordan before she could say more. "Jordan, if she is what you say she is, a witch, wouldn't you like to know for sure?"

A long silence followed. Jordan turned to face her cousin, "I don't know Lori. I'm too afraid to even think about it. I just don't know what to do. I think I just wanted someone to believe me, and now I've gotten you to at least agree that there is something weird going on. I hadn't thought about what to do next!" Jordan let out a shaky sigh, and shook her head.

Lori reached out and wrapped her arm around her cousin's shoulder. Lori's concern and comfort warmed Jordan. She was so grateful to have her cousin staying with her. She knew Lori would help her and together they would figure it all out. Lori had such an understanding way about her. She knew Lori would do everything she could. And she was sure that whatever they ended up doing, she would be safe with her cousin at her side. She knew everything was going to work out. Gosh, if only she could get her parents to move. That would solve everything. Then someone else could take care of Helga, someone older, and bigger. 'I'm too young to have such a big problem,' she thought.

They walked the remaining distance in silence. Jordan realized she was very tired. She was ready to curl up under the covers and close her eyes. Maybe tonight the bad dreams would not come to haunt her.

CHAPTER FOUR

A Feathery Friend

The next morning was sparking and bright. The birds were all singing at the tops of their lungs. A soft breeze floated in and ruffled the light curtains that framed Jordan's open bedroom window. Jordan slowly opened her eyes and allowed her body the luxury of a long full stretch, reaching her arms high above her head as her legs pushed out straight. Last night she had slept all night. She didn't have a single bad dream. Lying back on her pillow, her eyes drifted over to the bedroom window. A smile covered her face as she observed a little bird chasing a butterfly around the bush just outside. She rolled over in bed and was momentarily surprised to see her cousin sleeping soundly next to her.

Jordan jumped up to a sitting position. 'Oh,' she thought, 'I forgot Lori was here.' The memory of the night before came flooding back into her head.

Her sudden movement woke Lori up. Her cousin's sleepy eyes tried to focus on Jordan's face. Lori rubbed her eyes and propped herself up on her pillow. A tiny fluttering sound drew her attention to the open window. Looking toward the window, she noticed the little bird that Jordan had been watching earlier. "Jordan, look at that cute little bird. It looks like he's looking at us!"

Jordan gave a sideways glance at the bird, not really expecting to see anything different than what she had already been observing, but she was wrong. She almost laughed out loud with surprise and delight as her eyes locked onto the feathery little thing. He had moved from the bush to her window sill, and he was walking back and forth from side to side. His little head turned toward them as he did.

Jordan let out a squeal as she bounced to her knees on the bed. "He acts like he wants to come in, doesn't he," she said to her cousin.

"Yes, he does," Lori agreed. Both girls watched with joy as the tiny bird jumped up onto the screen, pushing his chest of fluffy feathers so tight against the screen that they could see some feathers push their way through.

"Wow," Jordan said, "he really does want in." She slid from the bed and slowly walked over to the window. She felt sure he would take flight once she got close to him. She was curious to see just how close she could get. She was at the window now, watching the bird tip his head back and forth as he nervously followed her movements. Suddenly, the birds wings fluttered hard and hit the screen with a loud swoosh. Jordan jumped. She could feel a gush of air from his small wings. She swirled around to Lori. "Pooh," she said in a disappointed tone. "I was almost …" Jordan's sentence was cut short by the surprised look on her cousin's face.

"Look, Jordan look!" Lori jumped off the edge of the bed and pointed toward the window.

Jordan turned back toward the window. The small bird had not flow away as she thought. Instead he had simply repositioned himself lower, down to Jordan's level. He was chirping loudly, and blinking his bright eyes at her. Jordan slowly reached out her hand. With one small finger she gently touched his tiny toes that barely poked through the screen wire. It was such a thrill for Jordan to be so close to a wild bird. She had always dreamed of walking through the forest among all the woodland creatures, petting a fawn, or snuggling a soft rabbit like in fairy tales. It made her sad that such creatures were afraid of her, but not this little guy. He didn't seem one bit afraid. "Lori, do you see this? He is letting me touch him!" Jordan tried to keep her voice soft so as not to frighten him away, but she was so excited it was very hard to stay calm.

Lori slowly made her way to her cousin's side. "Yes, Jordan I see. I see him. This is really strange. I have never seen anyone get this close to a wild bird without it being hurt or trapped. And even then, they have been so jumpy that it's almost impossible to touch them."

Jordan and Lori watched as the friendly bird pressed himself closer to the screen so the girls could both feel the velvety softness of his feathers. BANG! Jordan's bedroom door flew open and banged against the wall. It was Josh, Jordan's little brother. He was awake and ready to join his cousin and big sister for whatever fun they had planned for the day.

Josh was a happy four year old with chocolate pudding brown eyes surrounded by thick black eyelashes. His round face hid a smile that seemed eager to show itself. He loved his big sister, and loved playing with her. His sudden intrusion was unexpected, and both girls were alarmed by the invasion of this very special moment. Jordan jumped a good six inches off the floor and Lori let out a small squeal. Both girls turned to face the loud but short intruder.

"Shh. Josh, be quiet." Jordan waved her hand to signal him to stop right where he was.

Josh didn't understand why his sister seemed upset with him, but he stopped in his tracks. He wanted to let out a loud verbal protest, but the signal his sister had sent his way cautioned him to keep his response low. "What aw you doing?" he whispered. Josh quietly crossed the room to join both girls at the window. He looked out the window. With a curious frown on his face he looked up at his sister. "What aw you guys looking fo?" He didn't see anything of interest.

Both girls wore a disappointed look upon their faces. The fuzzy bird had disappeared. They both strained their eyes and stretched up on their toes as far as they could to see over the bush just outside the window, hoping that maybe he had moved to the yard or somewhere else in the bush. Sadly, he seemed to be nowhere in sight.

Jordan turned to face her little brother, anger flashing in her eyes. She put her hands on her hips and struggled to keep her voice down. "Josh, you scared him away," Jordan said.

Still very confused, Josh looked from the window to his sister and then to Lori. "Scawed who away Jodan? I didn't see anyone."

"It wasn't a person, it was a bird. He was right there on the screen, until you banged the door open."

Josh's eyes grew large with interest. "A biwd was on the scween? Why would a biwd be on the scwreen?" Josh looked at the window. His round face was filled with curiosity. His mouth formed a small circle, "Do you see him? What colow is he? I want to see him toooo." Josh placed his small hands on the window sill. Pulling himself up on his tiptoes he hoped to get a glimpse.

"I don't see him anywhewe. He's gone."

Jordan sighed, and stepped away from the window. Josh knew his sister was upset with him, and he was very sorry. Looking up at her, his big brown eyes filled with sadness. "I'm sowwy Jodan. I didn't know. I was just coming to get you and Lowi. Mom told me to. She said to tell you guys bwekfast is almost weddy." His eyes moistened. He didn't like to make his sister mad.

Jordan looked down at him and instantly felt sorry about getting so upset with him. She knew it wasn't his fault. There was no way he could have known about the bird. She put her hand out and patted her brother on the back. "It's okay Josh, you didn't know. But it sure was neat, wasn't it Lori?"

"It sure was," Lori said. "You should have seen him Josh. He got so close to the screen that we could touch his feathers."

Josh's eyes filled with excitement as he listened to the girls talk. He turned back to the window. "Maybe he'll come back if we caw him!" He pushed his face up to the screen and tried to whistle, but all he accomplished was blowing air. Then in a low voice he called out, "Here biwdy, biwdy, biwdy."

The vision was so funny that he had both Lori and Jordan giggling.

CHAPTER 5

Lori's Plan

After breakfast, all three kids played outside. Jordan felt relaxed and happy. Lori really wanted to talk to Jordan about Helga. What should they do next? The character in her mystery book always had a plan. They needed some sort of plan too. All day Lori's mind worked out some ideas that she would share with her cousin when they had some time alone, without Josh. That chance came sooner than Lori expected. The little boy next door invited Josh over to his house after lunch, and the girls had the rest of the day to themselves.

"Lori, why don't we take a blanket outside and put it under the tree in the back yard? We can build a tent out of some old sheets mom lets me play with. I have a new book I got for my birthday. It's a mystery and my friend that gave it to me says it's real good."

Lori agreed. "I love mysteries." The girls gathered up a few things and ran out the back door. Jordan dragged a big quilt under one arm and her new book under the other. She let the back door slam as she followed Lori, whose arms were full of sheets, clothespins, and pillows. Lori helped Jordan spread out the quilt and together they worked on attaching the sheets to some low branches of the big willow tree. They formed a perfect hide-away tent.

It was fun, and the girls laughed at the end result. "It may not look great, but we have a lot of room inside," Lori said, stepping back to examine the make shift tent. Lori grabbed a couple pillows and climbed inside. Jordan jumped in right behind her. Lori handed Jordan one of the pillows and both girls propped themselves into a comfortable position. Jordan grabbed the book and examined the cover. Lori decided this would be a good time to share her ideas about Helga. Lori knew Jordan would need some convincing, but she was sure she would do it.

"Jordan, I think I know how we can find out what Helga is really up to. And, if it is something awful I have an idea how we can get proof." Lori was excited about her plan.

Jordan dropped the book onto the quilt and looked over at her cousin. She slowly sat up. Jordan expected Lori would bring up the subject of Helga. She also knew that if she didn't listen to her cousin and let her help her solve the mystery about Helga, she would regret it. She had waited long enough. It was time to face her worst fears. It was time to do something to discover the truth about Helga. Jordan took a deep breath. "Okay, I'm listening. What do you think we should do?"

Lori was thrilled that Jordan didn't argue with her. She bounced to her knees and together the girls worked on Lori's plan. Lori started out by explaining they had to get a good close look at Helga, and they had to get pictures of her up close.

Jordan's eyes almost popped out of her head, "Lori, are you crazy? How do you think we can get a picture of her? We are going to have to stay completely out of sight. Besides, no one can get a close look at her. I already told you that I am the only one in the whole neighborhood who has seen her face to face.

Everyone else has only caught distant glimpses of her from the road."

"Jordan, we won't actually have to be all that close. Let me explain. I got a new camera for Christmas last year, and it has a zoom lens. Plus, I can turn the flash off. She won't even know we've taken her picture," Lori finished excitedly. Lori was very curious; she had to see Helga for herself. She thought about Jordan's encounter with Helga that day she followed the squirrels into her yard. Lori just wanted to get close enough to see her face. Helga had to have a face…everyone has a face…even bad people. She was sure that Jordan had somehow distorted her memory of that day.

Jordan sat back on the quilt, allowing Lori's words to soak in. Letting out a heavy sigh, she nodded in agreement. "Okay," Jordan replied. "How do you plan on getting her out of her house? We can't get a picture of her unless she's outside?"

"Well, I have an idea for that too. I thought we could go down there tonight, before it gets totally dark. We can hide in the weeds and make a noise of some kind, you know, like a puppy or something. And then when she comes out to see what it is she hears, we can take the picture, from a safe distance away of course."

As Jordan listened to her cousin's plan she could feel the all too familiar butterflies jumping around in her stomach. She wanted to do this, she kept telling herself. This is what she had always wanted to do, so why did she feel like she was going to be sick?

Lori continued with her plan for that night. She made a list of the things they would need to take with them. Jordan faced her cousin and nodded as the plan was laid out. Lori made it all sound so simple, and Jordan felt sure she would be safe with her cousin at her side. After all, if anything went wrong they would just run for home as fast as they could. Lori said they wouldn't have to get very close. It should work. The plan was ready to put into action.

"Okay Jordan, now let's have a look at that new book of yours. I'll start out reading first." Lori scooped the book up off the quilt and plopped back on her pillow.

Jordan observed how calm Lori was with it all, and even though Jordan did a good job of hiding the truth from Lori she couldn't hide it from herself. Her only comfort was that Lori wasn't afraid. Lori was going to be with her. Lori would take care of her, and she would keep her safe. Jordan allowed herself to relax. She laid back on her pillow and watched the sunbeams dance through the waving leaves of the big willow tree above them.

CHAPTER SIX

A Twilight Adventure

Everything was set. Jordan told her mom they were going next door to play hide-and-seek with her neighbor Sarah. They had Jordan's backpack stuffed with everything Lori said they would need, including flashlights and a camera. The last touch was to dress in dark clothes so they could hide in the heavy brush without being seen.

They were both very quiet on the way down the block. They did not take the road. Instead, they cut through the back part of the neighbor's yards. An old railroad track ran through the back border of everyone's property. The track wasn't used anymore by the railroad, and it was overgrown with tall weeds and small trees. It wasn't difficult for them to stay out of sight. Even so, Jordan could feel herself hunched over as if she needed to make herself shorter, smaller, and hopefully invisible. The semi-darkness of the evening was quickly turning into a deeper shade of black, and Jordan wondered if it had anything to do with the fact that they were now at the edge of Helga's yard.

Lori motioned for Jordan to follow her, and they both darted from the shelter of the weeds along side the track, through a small clearing, and then into the thicker weeds of Helga's backyard.

Jordan and Lori instantly sank down to their knees, wanting to stay out of sight. The instant Jordan entered the weeds she sensed something. What was it? Jordan looked over at Lori. Neither girl spoke to each other. Lori had instructed Jordan on several things as part of her plan, and being totally quiet was one of the things Lori said they must do. Otherwise their presence might be discovered

Both girls sat silently. Jordan's heart thumped hard in her chest. She tried to focus on what it was that felt so strange about being in Helga's yard. Was it warmer here? And what was that sound she heard? Had she heard it somewhere before? Then she knew. It was like waking from a dream. The clarity of what she was hearing came to her. It was someone humming a soft, strange tune. The sound filled her mind with questions, but she did not feel fear. When had that gone away? She felt herself relaxing, and in place of a worried frown she felt a smile spread across her face.

Her cousin Lori was dealing with her own mixture of curious feelings, many of which were similar to Jordan's. Lori could also hear the humming, and it was soothing. But the thing that kept Lori's mind most occupied were the big yellow eyes that she felt watching her. At first it frightened her, but now she could feel herself relaxing and she wondered why. Why was it that she could feel these huge weird eyes on her, and yet not feel frightened? It didn't make sense, but Lori was beginning to think that nothing about Helga made sense. Lori focused her gaze straight ahead. The eyes were there. She couldn't see them but she could feel them. She knew it was out there, and it was very close to them. She wondered if Jordan was right about them belonging to a black wolf.

Jordan's heart skipped a beat as a new sound came to her ears, so clear that she was sure it was only inches from her. This sound was even stranger than the others she'd heard, and could still hear in the distance. This was not music. This was something alive, she was sure of it. It sort of ticked and growled. No, it sounded more like a cat's purr. She felt every inch of her body go stiff. Now she was afraid. She was afraid to move. She was sure that even her heart had stopped beating as complete fear crept back in. She couldn't breathe, and her throat felt so tight that no scream could escape no matter how much she wanted it to.

She started slowly backing up. She knew she shouldn't move, but nothing on earth could have kept her from doing so. Chills covered her whole body, even her face. Her eyes were locked on the spot where the sound was coming from. She could hear it getting closer to her. Now her eyes grew wider as the weeds in front of her moved. No longer aware of anything except the thing coming toward her, Jordan spun around on her knees and started crawling as fast as she could to get out of the yard. She picked up speed and didn't give a thought to the cuts and scratches she was getting on her hands as she pushed on. Where was the clearing? Where were the railroad tracks? How far had she crawled? She was sure she was lost; she didn't know which way to go to get out of the yard. She stopped where she was, squeezed her eyes shut tight and listened. She listened for any hints of the thing that had been following her. She heard nothing. Maybe it was gone…. maybe she had gone far enough to escape it. She wanted to go home, but where was she? She was sure she should have come to the clearing by now. She looked around in every direction, but everything looked the same. She was definitely lost. Oh no, what about Lori! With a sinking heart, she suddenly realized she was not only lost, but alone. Lori had not followed her. Oh no, Jordan thought to herself. What have I done? Now what? I can't leave without Lori. What should I do?

All these problems jumped out of her head as a movement in the weeds brought her mind back to her present problem. Her ears filled with the same growling, purring sounds. Her eyes focused on the moving weeds in front of her as two small shining eyes stared out at her. Jordan wanted to jump up and run for home, screaming as loudly as her lungs would allow. The eyes came forward out of the grass, and entered the small space which she occupied. Fear gripped her like a trap and held her to the ground. She slammed her eyes shut, not willing to face the creature coming at her. Then, she heard a soft voice. It was saying something, but it was so soft and so distant that it was hard to hear. What was the voice saying? *Don't be afraid, don't be afraid.* Was it Lori? Had she followed her after all?

Jordan took a deep breath. Now the voice was closer; almost in her face. Her eyes were still shut tight and her body was tensed. "Lori, is that you?" Jordan whispered softly. She waited to hear Lori respond. There was nothing but silence. She couldn't hear anything, not even the growling sounds. They were gone. Jordan's eyes flew open and she pulled in a sharp breath. She was not expecting to see what laid only a couple of feet from her. A small creature poked its head out from the parting weeds. It crept into full view, now only inches from her. Its small eyes were surrounded by what looked like a black mask. It was a raccoon. He looked at her, and his head tilted to one side. Jordan relaxed. Looking at the small raccoon she judged it to be very young. And from the way it looked at her, she wondered if he was as frightened as she had been only minutes ago.

Maybe the voice came from him. Could that happen? No, no way. She knew that she needed to be cautious. Even though this raccoon was small and seemed friendly enough, he was a wild animal. She was sure he had a mouth full of sharp teeth. She held very still, waiting to see what he did next. Neither Jordan nor the raccoon took their eyes off each other. As Jordan studied him, he took one small step forward. Jordan slowly moved her hand out toward him. Very slowly, she inched it closer to him. She wanted to touch him, maybe he would even let her pet him. She decided the best thing to start with would be to let him smell her hand. That's always what she did with any dog or cat she wanted to make friends with. Why wouldn't it work with this little guy?

She held out her open hand and slowly moved it toward him. She was only inches from his nose. The raccoon did the last thing Jordan expected it to do. It moved toward her and gently placed his tiny paw into her outstretched hand.

Jordan was overcome with emotion. He wanted to be her friend. Wow! She moved her other hand out to pet him. First, she gently rubbed the top of his head and then she scratched him behind his ears. Instantly, a soft purring sound vibrated from him. He tilted his head and nearly laid it in her hand, as if asking for more. He wanted her to pet him. He liked it. A sigh of relief escaped her throat and a big smile spread across her face. Wow, she thought, I wonder if I could take you home with me. Softly she whispered, "I could keep you as my pet, and I already have the perfect name for you. I'll call you Sly."

Jordan pulled her backpack off her shoulders and settled

comfortably into the tall grass. She had momentarily forgotten where she was or why she was there. She scratched Sly behind his ears and under his chin. He was very friendly. He moved his paw out of her hand and slowly came closer to her. He gazed up at her and climbed up onto her legs. Jordan could not resist. She reached down and pulled the small furry raccoon into her arms. His soft ticking purring sound filled her ears and her smile broadened across her face.

The sound of a muffled scream shook Jordan back to reality. Oh no! Lori, I almost forgot about Lori!

CHAPTER SEVEN

Face To Face With Dark

L ori was on the far side of the yard, and she didn't realize she was alone. She was focused only on the eyes....only the eyes. She could see them now. Lori was terrified, too terrified to even hear the soft humming anymore. Her heart caught in her throat. The brief calmness she had felt just minutes earlier was gone. She wanted to scream out, no longer caring about Helga discovering them in her yard. She was certain that she had stopped breathing. It was as if every thought, every function of her body, everything in life, was frozen in this moment. The large yellow eyes were locked onto hers. She could not blink, and she could not turn her head away. She was trapped, and all the while the fierce eyes crept closer to her.

She needed help! Slowly, she forced her left arm to move stiffly from her side. She had to warn Jordan, maybe Jordan could go for help. Stretching out her arm as far as she could reach she groped around for her cousin. Alarm rang loudly in

Lori's mind as she realized Jordan wasn't there. She was gone! Now Lori knew she was all alone.

She had never fainted before, but she was sure she was about to now. As if she didn't have enough to deal with, a huge black spider appeared from somewhere above her. Lori hated spiders....and this one was very big and was right in her face. Then something unexpected happened. Out of the weeds an enormous black paw slashed out and smashed the insect into the ground.

A terrifying scream jumped from her throat. Her hands flew to her mouth in an effort to suppress it. She fell backward and landed hard onto the damp grass. The fierce eyes were bearing down on her. It must be the wolf. She could feel his hot breath hitting her face. Large white teeth were now visible. She felt her head spinning, and her stomach churning. Her hands started shaking out of control. Lori had never been more frightened in all her life.

Frozen to the ground with no hope for escape, Lori closed her eyes. She squeezed them shut as tight as she could and waited for the worst. Time stood still as she lay there in the dark. She waited, but nothing happened. Was it still there? Then she heard something, or someone. It was a voice. Someone was out there. Was it Helga? 'Maybe it's Jordan,' she hoped. She still could not open her eyes. The voice floated to her from over the tall grass. It seemed to be coming from a long way off. It was very soft, more like a whisper. What was it saying? She heard the same words repeated over and over.

"Don't be afraid of Dark. Don't be afraid of Dark." The words didn't make sense to her. She hadn't been afraid of the dark since she was little....that is ....until now. As she lay tense on the ground, the chanting words continued. Slowly she felt her body start to relax. The voice was tender and kind. Lori finally stopped shaking, and she felt warmth replace the cold. Again the words came out of the darkness, but this time it sounded different. This time it was closer, much closer. *"Don't be afraid of Dark, he will*

not hurt you. He will protect you. Dark killed the spider for you. Don't be afraid of Dark."

Not even thinking of the consequences, Lori sat up with a jolt. Her eyes flew open. "What …who…who is out there?" she whispered. Her eyes scanned the small grassy circle of space where she sat. There was nothing there, no more eyes, no more voice, nothing at all. For a moment she wondered if the voice could have come from the wolf.

Lori didn't wait around to find out. The wolf was gone, and this was her chance to get out of there. She had to find Jordan and get away, far away. She turned in the direction of the railroad tracks and started running. She did not even try to stay out of sight.

After Jordan heard Lori's scream, she jumped up. Sly had slipped off her lap and was at her feet, next to her back pack. Jordan was concerned about her cousin. She felt so ashamed that she had left her alone without a word, and now here she was playing with a sweet little raccoon while her cousin was dealing with who knows what.

She reached down and grabbed her backpack. Quickly, she surveyed the space at her feet for Sly. She had every intention of taking him home with her, but he was gone. Just like that he had scampered away. She was so upset, but there wasn't time to worry about him right now. She had to go find Lori. Lori needed her.

Jordan started running toward the middle of Helga's yard, to where she thought the scream had come from. Crouched down low, she ran as fast as she could. It was so dark, she couldn't see anything. She just kept running. She heard a rustling noise, and *CRASH*, the two girls knocked each other down.

Jordan didn't have a chance to say anything. She felt Lori grab her collar and drag her out of the yard. Once in the clearing, Lori pushed her index finger up to Jordan's lips. "Shh," Lori hissed. Then she grabbed Jordan by the arm and they ran the rest of the way home.

When they got to Jordan's yard Lori dropped to the ground. Gasping, she tried to catch her breath. "Jordan… are you … okay?" Lori asked with great difficulty.

Jordan was also breathing hard from the run. "Yes, I am." Jordan was bent over trying to catch her breath. She gazed down at Lori who was now lying on her back. "Lori, what happened? Did you see Helga? Did you take her picture?"

"No, I didn't see her. All I saw was the wolf. He was so close to me that I could feel his breath on my face."

Jordan's eyes nearly popped out of her head. "Whoa, he got that close to you and didn't eat you?" Jordan gasped.

Lori nodded her head up and down. "Yeah, for a minute I really did think he was going to do just that. But you know what he did instead? He smashed a giant spider that came out of the bushes. It was right in my face, and you know how much I hate spiders. And there was something else too, something really weird. I heard a voice." Lori just laid there staring up at the night sky, lost in the memory of that voice.

Jordan let a gasp escape her throat. "Lori, so did I. I heard a voice too. It kept saying, "D*on't be afraid; don't be afraid."* What did you hear it say?"

Lori's eyes flew to her cousin's and she sat up. "Jordan, are you sure? Are you sure that's exactly what you heard?"

"Yes, yes I'm sure. And the really funny thing is that it helped. I calmed down….and…"

Lori cut her off before she could go on. "Jordan, are you sure the voice didn't say more? Think hard. Could it have said, "Don't be afraid of Dark?""

Their conversation was cut short when they heard Jordan's mom calling to them. It was time to go inside.

Jordan looked up and called back to her mom. "We're coming mom. Just a minute." She sat down on the grass beside her cousin. She was feeling a bit guilty. Her experience in Helga's yard had been, well, fun! She had made friends with a raccoon...a baby raccoon. "Lori, where do you think the voice came from?"

Lori remained silent, staring off into the darkness. Jordan was worried about her. She reached out and put her hand on her cousin's shoulder. "Lori, are you alright? I mean, you're not hurt or anything are you?"

Lori didn't hesitate to reassure her cousin, "Oh I'm fine." Lori let out a short nervous laugh. "I'm fine. I am totally confused, but I'm fine. I just have to try and figure out what all this means. And I definitely think my plan needs some work, don't you?"

Both girls stood up, looked at each other, and began giggling. Maybe it was just a way of releasing some nervous tension. Whatever the reason, it felt good. By the time they walked in the back door they were laughing uncontrollably.

Jordan's mom was in the kitchen doing some last minute cleaning. "Well, I guess you two had a good time playing at Sara's."

Jordan and Lori stopped in their tracks. They looked over at Jordan's mom, and then at each other. Holding their sides, they ran from the kitchen laughing even harder.

They each showered and got ready for bed. When they got back into the bedroom, they found that Jordan's mom had popped them some popcorn and placed it and some drinks on a tray beside Jordan's bed. She knew this was one of Jordan's favorite snacks and even though it was late, she made an exception since she had company.

They jumped into bed, all cleaned up and excited to share everything they had experienced that night. The girls talked and snacked until late into the night. Jordan explained why she had left Lori alone in the yard. She told Lori she didn't mean to, and she really felt bad about Lori having that awful wolf get so close to her. Then she told Lori all about the cute little raccoon, and how she had named him Sly. "You know," Jordan said, "there was a moment there that I thought it was Sly talking, but then I know that's impossible, isn't it?"

Lori tensed up a bit. "Gosh Jordan, I don't know what to think. To be honest, I wondered the same thing about the wolf. I mean, he was right there in my face....and the voice became much stronger, louder, and closer. Then when I opened my eyes he was gone. There is no way an animal can talk. But if it wasn't him, then who was it?"

Jordan set the half-empty popcorn bowl over onto the tray, and both girls silently leaned back onto their pillows. Their minds filled with questions and curious thoughts about Helga and her yard. Sleep finally came to both girls, and so did the dreams. But these dreams were not as frightening to Jordan as they had been before. These dreams were filled with strange and almost magical creatures, all of which could talk. All of them led her to the same dark tunnel.

As Jordan and Lori fell deeper to sleep, someone else in Jordan's room was waking up. A curious little stowaway cautiously climbed out of Jordan's backpack and peered around her room.

CHAPTER EIGHT

An Uninvited Guest

Bright light poured in through Jordan's bedroom window. Both girls woke up at the same time. Something woke them. What was it?

Jordan slowly pulled herself up and threw back the covers. Lori did the same, and they both looked around the room. Neither girl was prepared for the sight that awaited them. Jordan's room was a disaster. It looked like someone had taken the popcorn bowl and dumped it upside down in the middle of her floor. There were clothes tossed about everywhere, and even some toys pulled down from her bookcase. There were books and crayons scattered all over. What had been left of their drinks were now puddles on the carpet.

"This is not good! What happened? Who made this mess? My mom is going to have a fit!" Jordan didn't know what to do. She wanted to cry. She wanted to run and tell her mom she didn't do it, but who did do it....and why? 'That's the first question mom will ask me. I can hear her now,' she thought. 'If you didn't do this Jordan, then tell me who did?'

"Lori, did you see me walk in my sleep last night? I mean, I don't think I have ever done that before, but I have a friend who swears she does it all the time."

"I don't know…. I don't know what to think. I didn't hear anything last night, did you?" Lori continued to scan the mess in Jordan's room.

Jordan shook her head back and forth. "No, I slept better than I have in weeks. I didn't hear a thing. What do you think happened? Maybe Helga followed us home last night and came into my room." Jordan let that thought sink in. Her eyes grew large and her mouth flew open. "Oh my gosh! You don't think that's what happened do you Lori?" Jordan was about to have a major melt down.

Lori jumped out of bed and surveyed the damage. Jordan's question made Lori stop in her tracks. "No way. Your parents always lock up at night, don't they? She couldn't get in through a locked door. And besides, why would she? No, I don't think so." However, Jordan's question did make Lori wonder if Helga could have something to do with this. Maybe Helga saw them in her yard last night and this was her way of saying, *stay out of my yard.*

Jordan was breathing fast and she started walking back and forth. "What are we going to do about this?" She turned to her cousin. "What are we going to do?"

Lori forced herself to stop thinking about Helga. "Surely there is an explanation for all this. We'll figure it out. But for now, we need to do something about this mess. Jordan, I think we should just clean everything up before your mom sees it. We don't want your mom upset with us, and we don't know what happened. For now let's just keep this to ourselves. I'm sure we'll figure it out, somehow. There has to be an explanation. And besides, nothing seems to be broken or damaged. It's just a mess, and we can fix that."

Jordan liked that idea, "Yeah, I don't think anything is broken. Ok, let's do it." Together, the girls worked very fast and very hard. They quietly got a wet towel from the bathroom and cleaned up the carpet. Next, they worked on picking up all the clothes, toys, and popcorn.

They were almost finished when they heard Josh knock at the bedroom door. His small voice called out to them. "Jodan… Lowi, aw you awake?"

Jordan and Lori froze, and their eyes flew to the door. "At least he knocked this time," Lori whispered. She was rewarded with a quick smile from Jordan. Lori let out a giggle and they both ran to the door to open it. With big smiles plastered on their faces, they squeezed out the door and closed it behind them.

Josh was curious and tried to peek into the room before they shut the door. "Good morning Josh," Lori said smiling down at her young cousin.

Josh quickly forgot about the room and smiled up at Lori. "Mom said fo me to get you guys. It's time fo bweakfast." With that said, he ran up the hall to the kitchen.

Jordan had a hard time hiding her emotions at breakfast. She pushed her pancakes around on her plate. Her mom knew she loved pancakes and asked, "Jordan, aren't you hungry this morning? Did that late night snack fill you up too much?"

The mention of the snacks made her really jumpy. "Oh no… ..I mean yes. I mean…..wow mom, we loved the popcorn and drinks. Thank you so much."

"Yes Aunt Michelle, we really enjoyed it. We didn't finish it all, oh, I mean, we did finish it all……and it was great." Lori tried to save the moment, but only made things worse.

"You two are up to something. What is it?" Jordan's mom questioned. She looked at the two girls, waiting for an answer. Jordan did not know what to say. Her eyes went to Lori, pleading for help.

"Well, it's my fault Aunt Michelle. When I jumped out of bed this morning I accidentally bumped the tray and spilled the left over popcorn. But we already cleaned everything up, I mean, cleaned it up."

"Yeah, we cleaned it up mom, and we are very sorry." Jordan let out a deep breath. She was relieved that Lori had jumped in.

Jordan's mom sensed that there might be more to the story, but she let it go. The conversation turned to the events planned for the day and it was decided that Josh and the girls would play board games outside. Josh thought the tent the girls had made the day before looked like a lot of fun. He talked them into setting up his little tent and playing games with him in it. Jordan really wanted to spend time alone with Lori, but it would have to wait.

The girls went back to Jordan's room to get the games and a few other things. Lori filled her arms with board games while Jordan grabbed her backpack and two pillows. Her book was still in her backpack, and she thought maybe they would have some time to read it later. She took an extra moment to pick up the last of the popcorn and throw it away. Confident that her room looked clean, they headed for the back yard. Josh was already outside with his tent, waiting for them to help him with it.

It didn't take long to set up the tiny tent. Lori stood back while Jordan and Josh climbed in. She wondered if there would be room for all three of them to get inside and still have enough room to play games. She followed her cousins inside.

It was a tight fit, but the morning was cool. They were very comfortable inside. Pillows, games, and snacks pushed against the edges. They had everything they needed. They started out with clue, and they let Josh go first. The girls grabbed their pillows and put them in place.

"Hey, where's my piwwow? Didn't you bwing one fo me?" Josh asked with a deep frown on his round face. "Oh well, that's okay. I'll just use Jodan's backpack," he said. He reached over, grabbed the strap, and dragged the backpack toward him. Then he picked it up and placed it behind him so he could lean back on it. "Okay, I'm weddy too." He looked very satisfied as he leaned back on the backpack, making himself comfy.

They had only been playing a short time when they all three heard a strange noise. It was a snarling squeak of a noise. They looked at one another, wondering who made the noise. Both girls settled their eyes on Josh.

"Don't wook at me. I didn't do it. I didn't do anything."

"Josh, you did too make that noise! It came from you," his sister insisted.

"Uh-uh, I did not!" he demanded.

"What ever you say Josh. Just don't do it again, okay," his sister requested.

They went back to their game and played for a few more minutes. Suddenly, Josh paused. "Jodan, yo backpack is too lumpy, I need a weal piwwow." He turned around and poked at her backpack, trying to make it more comfortable. As he did, they heard the noise again. This time all three children stared at Jordan's backpack.

"Jodan, what do you have in yo backpack? It's moving, wook!" Josh exclaimed, pointing his short finger in the direction of the bag.

A squeaking sound came sharp and loud from inside the bag, and all three kids jumped up. Unfortunately, the tent was too small to stand up in and everyone fell all over each other. No one wanted to be very close to the backpack and all of them searched for the door, which had been zipped shut. The tent was not staked down. The activity from inside caused it to first bounce around, and then roll across the yard. It looked more like a big beach ball...a beach ball with three screaming children inside it. Down the sloping yard they rolled, all the while Lori continued to try to get a hold of the zipper and open the door.

Rippp...a tearing sound and daylight. They were free. Jordan was the first to fall out the hole that had ripped open. She rolled out across the yard. Her backpack followed her. She finally landed on her back, and her backpack bounced up on top of her stomach. In a flash of fur a tiny raccoon jumped from the backpack and onto the ground. Sly ran across the yard and was out of sight in seconds.

Josh and Lori were now sprawled across the yard several feet apart. The small tent was never going to be a tent again. It lay on the ground like a deflated balloon.

Jordan was stunned. Sly had somehow gotten into her backpack last night. He had come home with her. She fell back onto the grass, laughing. She couldn't believe it. He had come home with her. She rolled over and saw Lori and Josh still lying on the ground where they had landed. She jumped up and ran to them, still laughing. Josh and Lori looked up at her as if she were nuts.

"What is so funny?" Lori asked, very confused. Lori and Josh stood up and brushed off their clothes. "What's the matter with you?"

Jordan could not explain with her little brother right there. She wanted to say something, but she couldn't think of what, so she just laughed harder.

Josh looked over at his tent and at all the games and stuff scattered all over the yard and started to cry. "My tent is bwoken. Wook at my tent! What happened Jodan, what happened?"

Jordan instantly felt bad for her little brother. "It's okay Josh, don't cry. Everything will be okay. Lori and I will pick everything up, don't you worry about it. Just go inside and we'll explain everything to mom. Don't say anything to her yet. Give us a chance to clean all this up first, okay?" Jordan tried to comfort her little brother.

"But what happened? What made that noise? What was in yo backpack?" He was sure something was going on, and he wanted to be included.

She was going to have to tell him something. He had heard the noises; he knew something had been in her backpack.

"Josh, just go in the house. I promise if you don't say anything to mom about this, I will tell you...but later. I promise." He really wasn't in the mood to argue. He was ready to go inside. As he turned toward the house, Jordan patted him on the back. Both girls watched as a ruffled little Josh gave up and walked away, temporarily satisfied to not have to help clean up.

The minute he was inside the back door Jordan spun around to face her cousin. "Lori, you're not going to believe this. It was Sly…..he was in my backpack!" Jordan was so excited, she started laughing again.

"Who is Sly? Oh Sly, the raccoon from last night. Are you sure? How could that have happened?" Lori asked.

"I don't know, but somehow last night he must have climbed in it. He was in my room with us all night."

Lori's eyes grew large. "That's who made the mess in your room."

"Yes, I am sure of it. Boy does that ever make me feel better. I just knew it was Helga. I was sure of it. I wish he wouldn't have run away. I wanted to hold him; I wanted to show him to you. You would love him. He is so cute, and so soft. I feel just awful about him being frightened like that. I mean, Josh laid on him and was even punching on my backpack. It must have scared him. I sure hope he isn't hurt. I feel so awful. I need to hold him. I need to know he's okay. We have to go back to Helga's tonight." Jordan's face was covered with a worried frown. "Lori, we have to. I know he wants to be with me; otherwise he wouldn't have gotten in my backpack. And now he's back in that awful yard. We have to save him."

"But Jordan, how can you be sure that's where he is? He could be anywhere by now." Lori tried to make her cousin think about what she was saying. "After all, this is a raccoon…just a little raccoon. It's not like a dog, or a cat. He's not your pet."

"Yes he is. He is my pet, or he will be if we can just go get him. I saw him run toward Helga's yard. I know he's there, and I know we can find him."

Lori was surprised that Jordan didn't seem worried about going back…back to that weed patch…back to the dark. Maybe

Jordan wasn't worried, but Lori was. She didn't know if she was ready for that, or if she would ever be ready. She didn't want to let her cousin know that she was a little afraid. She didn't even want to admit that to herself, much less Jordan. She was the older of the two and she should not be afraid, especially if Jordan wasn't. Taking a deep breath, Lori turned away from her cousin and started picking up the games. "We better get this mess cleaned up before your mom sees it. She will be wondering why Josh went inside without us."

"Okay, sure. So when do you want to go? Maybe this time we can go down before dark. That would be much better don't you think?" Jordan joined Lori in picking up the yard.

'Okay,' Lori thought. 'She isn't anymore eager than I am about stepping back into Helga's yard. She just wants to get Sly.' That gave Lori an idea. "Jordan, maybe we can get Sly without going into Helga's yard. We could save some of our dinner from tonight and take it with us. We could stay just at the edge of her yard and use the food as bait." Lori was proud of her idea. It would work. Jordan could get Sly back and Lori would not have to admit she didn't want to go into the yard again.

Jordan loved the idea. "Yeah, and if we go right after dinner it will still be daylight. It should work, right? He should come to us if we offer him food. Yeah, it will work." Jordan smiled, happy to have some sort of a plan and happy to know she was going to save Sly from Helga.

CHAPER NINE

Trapped In Helga's House

After dinner was over the girls helped Jordan's mom clean up and they ran back to Jordan's room. Both of them pulled napkins full of tasty leftovers out of their pockets for Sly. They had already told Jordan's mom that they were going over to Sara's to watch a movie and would be home right after it was over.

They both jumped when they heard a loud knock on her bedroom door. Jordan jammed her napkin of food back into her pocket and ran to the door. It was Josh, and he bounced into her room before she could block him from entering. "Josh, we're going to Sara's house. What do you want?" Jordan wanted to leave, and she wanted to get this over with before dark.

Josh looked up at his sister with a questioning gaze. "Jodan, you said you would tell me what made that noise. What was in yo backpack? You promised. You said if I didn't say anything to mom, you would tell me...remembo?"

Jordan gave a look of frustration to her cousin and then to

Josh. "Okay I know, but can I tell you tomorrow? We really need to get over to Sara's."

"No," he demanded, "tell me now. What was it? Was it a cat? I saw a cat in the back yawd yestewday, and I tried to catch it, but it ran fastew than me and got away. Is that what it was?" He watched his sisters face with anticipation.

Jordan's face changed from frustration to joy. "Oh yes! How did you guess? It was a cat. Somehow it got in my backpack, maybe while we were setting up the tent. Anyway, that's what it was. Now, we have to go." She finished in a rush and opened her door for him to exit.

"Wow, I knew it was that cat. Maybe we can catch him tomowow. And maybe mom will let me keep him. Do you think mom will let me have a cat Jodan? Do you?"

"I don't know Josh, maybe. Good night. We'll see you in the morning." This time she guided him out her door and closed it behind him.

Once Josh had gone down the hall to his room, Jordan shoved the leftovers into her backpack and slung it over her shoulder. Lori led the way down the hall to the back door. They scurried across the yard and into the cover of the small trees that lined the railroad tracks. They didn't stop until they reached the small clearing at the edge of Helga's yard.

Lori sat down in the grass and reached for Jordan's backpack. She started pulling out the food scraps they had saved from dinner. Neither one of the girls felt very comfortable being this close to Helga's place again, but Lori was confident this wouldn't take very long. She placed several pieces of food in the tall grass just inside Helga's yard. Now all they had to do was wait. They knew they must remain very quiet for several reasons. They did not want to alert Helga that they were there, and they did not want to frighten off Sly. They had to get him close enough so they could pick him up. And of course there was another reason...and that reason had big yellow eyes. Lori took in a deep breath, and then released it slowly. Everything would be okay. They were not going to go in the yard, so everything would be okay. Lori closed her eyes and tried to relax.

Jordan stayed watchful; she knew Sly was in there somewhere. She hoped he would be able to smell the food they brought. She wondered what a raccoon's favorite food was, and hoped the hamburger and hot dog would do the trick. It was a very still night. There was no breeze at all and the evening air was cool for August. Jordan closed her eyes and pictured Sly. She imagined him playing with a butterfly, trying to catch it in his small paws. He was so cute.

A very soft melody from deep within the brush crept over the top of the grass and trees. It moved toward them, slow and soft the way fog does over a lake on a still night. One would hardly notice it moving at all, it was so slow, and so soft. It soothed them into a trance, and neither one of the girls were even aware they were hearing it.

Lori started humming along, and Jordan did the same. They were each still sitting there in the grass, then both girls closed their eyes and drifted off to sleep.

It was like a dream. Lori saw smoky images of a black wolf. He was not frightening, but there was something odd about the way he looked at her. Almost like he understood she was afraid of him and it made him sad. She could see tears in his eyes... his big yellow eyes. And then the voice again, but this time it was different. It was much deeper and stronger. *"Don't be afraid of Dark. I would never harm you. I am a protector. I could never hurt you."*

Jordan was also experiencing a series of dreams. First she saw Sly. He came bouncing up to her and jumped into her arms. She hugged him and scratched him behind his ears. She was quickly rewarded by his loud, happy purring. As she held him, a cloudy image approached her. At first it was so blurry that it looked like a black rain cloud coming to her...but then it slowly started taking shape....the shape of a shaggy black cloak of a dress, with a torn, black hood. Oh no, it was Helga. Jordan felt herself tense up.   She wanted to open her eyes, she wanted to wake up, and she really wanted to run away. 'It's only a dream,' she told herself. 'It's only a dream.' As the black shapeless woman approached her she tried to back up, but she was rooted to the ground. There would be no escape this time. Helga came closer, and closer. Now Jordan could see the claw-like hands. One of those hands reached up and out towards Jordan. Frozen like a popsicle, all Jordan could do was stare out at …at…Helga. Helga was standing right in front of her. "Go away," Jordan moaned, pushing her hands out in front of her as if she were shielding herself from Helga's outstretched hand. Then she heard something, whimpering, someone was crying. Could it be Helga? Maybe it was her own sobbing she heard. No, she wasn't crying. She was dreaming, wasn't she? If it was Helga, why would she be crying? Now a voice came to Jordan. Very clearly it said, *"Don't be afraid. I would never hurt you. You don't need to be afraid of me. I know my appearance is strange."* Helga reached out her scraggly hand toward Sly, who stretched his head up to allow her to gently pet him.

Suddenly the dream was over, and the two cousins popped their eyes open at the same time. They felt extremely groggy, like when you first wake up in the morning.

Lori was the first to speak. She turned toward her cousin, blinked her eyes, and yawned. She could tell Jordan looked droopy eyed too. "Jordan, did you fall asleep? I think I did, and I even had a dream. Did you, I mean, did you have a dream too?"

Jordan nodded her head up and down. She let her mind replay the dream. "Yes, yes Lori I did have a dream. It was very weird. At first I was playing with Sly. It was so neat, but then I saw Helga. She came up to me and I thought she was going to hurt me, but then, well she seemed sad. She was sad because I was afraid of her. That's what she said to me. This is too creepy." Jordan sat there shaking her head back and forth. "What was your dream like?"

Lori lowered her voice. "In my dream I saw the yellowed eyed wolf. He came out of a fuzzy black fog, and he looked sad too. In fact I think he was crying."

"Oh my gosh, I forgot that part. Helga was crying too. Yeah, I mean, well yeah, she was sobbing. I couldn't see her face, but I could hear her, and she reached out to pet Sly. What do you think it means Lori? How could we both fall asleep at the same time, and both dream about them. The two things we are most afraid of?"

The girls sat close to each other in silence for a few minutes, both hearing those words over and over in their heads.

Lori shook her head, trying to clear the memory of it away. "It doesn't matter. We are here to get Sly and get out of here. Let's just do what we came here to do." She peered into the weeds to check on the food she had placed there. She moved her head down closer to the grass and blinked her eyes. She couldn't see anything very well. Then she realized why. It was dark, as black as the deepest night could get. "Jordan, it's dark. We must have slept for…well…I don't know how long, but long enough for night to come."

"Gads, you're right. I didn't even notice it. I don't really want to be here in the dark. That's why we came early. Now what are we going to do?" Jordan expected her cousin to have an answer to this new and unexpected problem.

"Well, why don't we go back home and try again tomorrow? We could come down in the morning, as soon as we can slip away without Josh noticing? How about that?"

Jordan sat beside her in silence. She wanted to find Sly tonight. She wanted to take him home with her now. And she didn't want to leave him here, not even for one night. Jordan could picture his frightened little face as he jumped out of her backpack. She so badly wanted a chance to hold him, to take care of him. "Lori, I want to find Sly tonight. I know he's here, and close by. I just know it. I want to go home too, but I want to get Sly first. Please? Can't we try, just for a little while?" Jordan was almost crying. She pulled her hands up to her face.

Lori wiggled around in the grass. She didn't want to be here…she just didn't, but Jordan did. And she had to confess, she had not felt the uneasy sensation of anything or anyone watching them as she had before. Lori sucked in a deep breath. "Okay Jordan, okay. We will give Sly a chance. But we must not fall asleep like that again, and we must stay right here together. Remember, we talked about this. You do not move away from me, and I will not move away from you. Just to make sure, it's time to do what we talked about.

Jordan nodded and reached into her backpack. Earlier that day when they worked out their plan, they both agreed they would tie themselves together. Jordan pulled out the short piece of rope and handed one end of it to Lori. The other end she tied around her waist. Lori was doing the same with her end of the rope. They had about three feet of slack between them. This gave them just enough space to move around comfortably.

"I am really sorry about last night," Jordan said. "I just couldn't help it. I was afraid that something was after us, and I really thought you had followed me. Really, I did."

Lori knew her cousin couldn't help what happened when she moved to the other side of the yard the night before. She understood that being in Helga's yard meant that many strange things could and probably would happen. So just to be safe she came up with this idea. It made her feel much better knowing they would be together, no matter what. "I know Jordan, don't worry about it. We are stuck with each other now, no matter what."

Jordan felt goose bumps travel across her arms and legs. She had the feeling that Lori wanted to say more, but didn't. She didn't want to think about it. All she wanted to do was find Sly. 'Come on Sly,' she thought to herself. 'Come on out of there. Come to me, and I will take good care of you. I promise.'

The next few moments passed in silence, and then Jordan

heard a noise. It was a rustling sound coming from the weeds right in front of them. Both girls heard it. They focused their eyes on the spot where they had placed the food.

Jordan gave a small excited jump of joy as she saw a tiny paw reach out and snatch a scrap of food. "It's him! It's Sly," she chirped. He did come, she knew he would. Jordan repositioned herself and reached out her arms, opening her hands so she could get a hold of him as soon as he came out far enough.

Lori sat a couple more tidbits of food on the grass in front of Jordan. They needed him to come out into the open. Lori was worried that if they reached into the weeds for him, he would get away before they caught him. She placed a warning hand on Jordan's shoulder to hold her back. She knew it was hard for her cousin; she was so excited to be this close to the raccoon.

Jordan held herself back, watching the grass wiggle about. She waited. First came his little black nose. It twitched back and forth smelling the new snack. Then one paw and then the next. Now his face pushed out, parting the grass. He stopped and looked up at Jordan. She was sure he had a smile on his face. "Sly, there you are. I've been waiting for you. Come on, come on out. We won't hurt you," Jordan coaxed softly.

Lori's eyes grew large as she watched the adorable tiny raccoon come out from the shelter of the weeds. He was looking at Jordan as if he remembered her. She saw him pick up the bit of food and sit up on his back legs. He was close enough to Jordan that he was leaning up against her legs. She watched as he used his paws like small hands, turning the piece of hotdog over and over while nibbling at the edges. It was amazing. He was so cute. "Oh Jordan, look at him, he wants to be close to you." Lori was smiling. It felt good after the tension she had felt all evening.

Jordan had not picked Sly up as she had planned. He seemed happy to be with her, and she loved watching him eat the hotdog, so she and Lori relaxed and enjoyed the moment. After the hotdog was gone, Sly looked at Lori and then back at Jordan. "Do you think he wants more?" Lori asked. She reached for the backpack to get him more. Sly followed her movements, and when he saw the unfriendly backpack he froze. Neither girl noticed the tension on his face or the stiffness of his body. Two seconds later he growled a low sound and headed for the weeds.

"No, no Sly, it's okay. No!" Jordan cried out. She jumped up and without thinking ran after Sly.

It only took seconds for the short rope to grow tight and pull hard on Lori's waist. Her mouth opened to scream at Jordan to stop, but it was too late. Jordan was on a mission and not even the rope could stop her. Even though Lori was 16 months older than Jordan there wasn't too much difference in their size. Lori was being dragged along, and she knew she needed to get her feet under her or she'd be dragged to who knows where.

Jordan hardly felt the rope pulling at her waist. She knew she had to keep up with Sly. She had to get close enough to catch him. She couldn't lose sight of him or he would be gone. He was scared, scared of her backpack. She was mad at herself for not thinking of that. She shouldn't have brought it with her. She tripped, and hurried to regain her footing. This slight pause gave Lori the chance she needed to jump to her feet. Now she ran hard to keep up with Jordan.

Everything was happening so fast. Lori felt as if they had been running for five minutes. Where were they? It was so dark. Suddenly Jordan stopped. Her whole body stood straight and stiff. Sly had run to Helga's house, and Jordan saw him take one long leap right into her open door, which was now only inches in front of her.

Lori didn't realize her cousin had stopped, and she plowed right into the back of her. The force caused both girls to tumble straight inside Helga's house.

Jordan hit the ground hard, and her cousin landed on top of her. Fear gripped Jordan by the throat. 'Oh my gosh,' she thought. 'We are in Helga's house. Oh my gosh! We have got to get out of here!'

Lori blinked her eyes. She was surrounded by total darkness.

She blinked her eyes again, but it did no good. It was as if her eyes were shut. She couldn't see anything. "Jordan," she whispered. "Are you there?" She stretched out her hands and groped around for her cousin.

"Yes," Jordan whispered. "You're sitting on top of me!"

Lori immediately moved over and reached out to help Jordan sit up. "Oh I'm sorry Jordan. I can't see anything. Where are we?"

Jordan managed to find Lori's mouth with her hands, which she quickly covered to muffle Lori's words. She moved her hands to each side of Lori's head. Moving in close, she whispered into her cousin's ear. "We are in Helga's house, and we need to get out of here...now!"

Alarm bolted through Lori's body. How on earth did they end up in Helga's house? 'Oh no! This is not good,' Lori thought. She struggled to stand up, but they were both tangled up in the rope. Lori's fingers searched for the knot. Silently Jordan joined in the effort, but the knots were so tight and her hands were shaking so badly she wasn't having any luck.

Lori felt certain that even if they stayed tied together they could run away and get out of here, if they could just see. Instinctively Lori's head darted back and forth, thinking she could find the door. But all she could see was blackness, nothing but blackness. 'How could it be so dark in here? What are we going to do?' Both girls were so scared. They needed to be able to communicate with each other, to find a way out. But neither one of them dared to speak.

Suddenly Lori's thoughts froze. Something was wrong; a creepy feeling seeped into her mind. She could feel air moving, as if a door or window had suddenly opened. She felt her head spinning and her stomach churning. Her hands started shaking out of control. The feeling was familiar. It was the wolf. She could feel his eyes on her back.

Jordan felt the change in the room as well, and she felt the tension in her cousin. They were still sitting on the floor, very close to each other.

Lori did not want too, but she couldn't help it. She felt her head slowly turn. As she did, a very slight glow of light shined out from the far side of the room. A sharp intake of breath caught in her throat as her eyes found what they were looking for. His eyes were so bright, and it was that brightness that caused the room to light up. 'No, please no. Go away,' Lori wanted to scream at him. 'Go away,' her mind pleaded.

Jordan looked over at the far side of the room. "AAHHHH", Jordan let a scream break the silence. It filled the room so full that it echoed back and forth off the walls.

The two girls dug their feet into the floor and pushed themselves backward, away from the frightening animal. They kept pushing until they ran into something. There was no time to see what it was. As if one girl knew what the other was thinking, they worked together to press their backs against the hard surface behind them and used it to help them stand up. Lori was sure she would feel better if she could be on her feet, ready to run at the first opportunity. The sound of their breathing filled the room. Well, it almost filled the room….there was another sound.

Again, it was the voice…but it did not come from far away as it usually did. This time it was very clear and very close. It sounded like it was coming from the same corner of the room where the black wolf was. *"Why are you still afraid of dark? I told you, he is my protector. He is the protector of all, and he will not hurt you."*

Lori thought for a moment about what the voice had said. Dark…don't be afraid of dark. That's what she heard that first night. Suddenly, it all made sense. Dark must be his name. Helga has a pet wolf, and his name is Dark, and the voice must belong to Helga. She must be here with them. She must be standing beside the wolf. Helga knew they were in her yard last night. This wasn't good. Was Helga mad at them? She did not hear anger in her voice. In fact, there was no feeling in the voice at all. It did not sound mad, or insistent. It was flat and to the point.

Lori mustered up every ounce of courage she could find, and when she spoke her voice was strong and clear. "We want to leave. Just make him …just make Dark go away." She was hoping and praying that she sounded strong enough for Helga to believe her to be brave.

The reply that came back to them was not what they expected.

"Not until you listen to me. I need you. I cannot let you leave yet."

Jordan suddenly found her voice, and she nearly screamed out at the top of her lungs. "Helga, I know what you are, and if you don't let us go my dad will come and get you. He will. If you don't let us go, you will be in big trouble." She finished with a quivering sob. "Please let us go." Tears streamed down her face.

"My name is not Helga, and I am not a witch! I am a Guardian. You must not let my present appearance frighten you! I need your help. I am not going to hurt you." Again, the voice held no emotion.

Lori's mind was flying with questions. Jordan did not say she was a witch….why would Helga say that? And what did she mean, she needed help? Help from them? What did she mean?

"I will tell you what I mean. I will tell you everything when the time is right. You must help me. You are the only ones who can help me, and I can prove to you that I am not going to hurt you. Jordan, remember that day when you followed the squirrels into my yard? Remember the car? Remember being lifted out from its path? It was me who saved you that day. I would never harm you or anyone. That's not what a Guardian does." The voice trailed off, and a sudden feeling of sadness filled the room. *"I have lost my charm, and if you refuse to help me, I will…"* Dark let out a tiny whimper and laid down on the floor, never taking his eyes off the girls.

Jordan's eyes grew large. Her mouth opened and formed a tight circle. She stopped crying. How, how could she know about that day, and how could she know my name? Jordan tried to speak her thoughts out loud. "How did you…?" Her words fell away in silence. She stood there, not moving. She no longer knew what to say, or what to think.

Lori was amazed. Helga had responded to what Lori had been thinking. She had not asked her questions out loud. How did Helga know? How could Helga know what she was thinking?

The tension was so great, and for two young girls it was enormous. But out of the shadows came a tiny figure. It scampered across the floor toward the girls. It was Sly. He stopped at Jordan's feet and waited, as if he knew she was going to pick him up. It broke the tension in the room. Jordan looked down at his sweet face. She reached down for Sly and pulled him into her arms. He seemed happy to be there. The girls looked at each other in silence, both wondering what was going to happen next.

A squeaking sound creaked from across the room. A soft moon beam sprang into the darkness from an opening. It was a door; an open door. The girls did not look around or wait for permission. They scurried across the room still tied together, holding on tightly to Sly and to each other. They ran all the way home.

CHAPTER TEN

What Does Helga Want?

When the girls got home, they moved through the house very quietly. Jordan had already brought the pet taxi up from storage earlier that day, with high hopes she would have Sly with her by tonight. That part of the night was the only thing that had worked out. The rest of the creepy events were almost a blur. Jordan's mind raced with so many questions. She had so many things she wanted to ask Lori about, but didn't know which question to start with. Did they really go inside Helga's house? Had they really talked to her? After all, they never did actually see her.

Jordan closed her bedroom door gently, switched on her bedside lamp, and placed Sly on the floor. She leaned back against the bedroom door, exhausted.

They both worked in silence, hurrying to get Sly's bed ready for him and getting themselves ready for bed. They were so tired, and yet neither one of them were sleepy. Jordan placed a small towel in the pet taxi for Sly to sleep on, but she didn't have the heart to put him inside it. Instead, she allowed him to curiously inspect her room, hoping he would not destroy it again.

Lori broke the silence at last by asking perhaps the spookiest question of all. "Jordan, do you think Helga can read our thoughts? I have heard of people who can do that. Some of the things she said to us we had not said out loud?" Lori waited for Jordan's response.

Jordan thought for a minute. She couldn't remember exactly what was said by whom. She remembered that Helga said she wasn't a witch, and that she wanted their help, and...about that day she almost got hit by that car. That one really had her confused. "What do you mean Lori? Why do you think she can do that?" Jordan watched Sly grab a hold of her bedspread and climb up on top of her bed.

"Well," Lori began, pacing back and forth on the soft carpet. "She told you she wasn't a witch. You hadn't said anything to her about being a witch. How would she know about that? And I've been thinking about what she meant by needing our help. Her words were...something about she would tell us exactly what she meant when the time was right, or something like that. Anyway, it was as if she knew what I was thinking. Do you remember if you were thinking about her being a witch? Do you?" Lori waited.

"Lori," Jordan said as she turned to face her cousin, "That is always what I'm thinking, always. Especially when I am anywhere near her yard...or in her house. Oh my gosh! I still can't believe we were in her house."

"Yeah, that's something else I wondered about. Why would you go in her house, even for Sly? I can't believe you did that." Lori threw her arms in the air.

"I didn't want to go in Helga's house. You pushed us in. I tried to stop, as soon as I saw Sly leap in through her front door," Jordan replied in a rush of words.

"Ohhhh, well, that explains that." Lori said with a look of understanding on her face.

"Lori, none of this makes sense to me. Why would a wicked looking woman like Helga, or whatever her name is, need our help? What could we do for her that she couldn't do herself? And why us? Do you think she's trying to trick us? And did you hear what she said she was? She said she was a Guardian, and she lost her charm. What does that mean? The only charms I know of are the ones on charm bracelets. What do you think she was talking about?" Jordan climbed up on her bed to play with Sly. He was happily rolling around, playing with one of her stuffed animals. "There are so many weird things going on, like when we were at the edge of her yard, and we fell asleep sitting up. I have never done anything like that before. It's like she put a spell on us. That is too weird."

"I've been thinking about that too. I think Helga did that to us. I don't know how, but I'll bet she did it. She made us fall asleep, but she didn't hurt us. She wanted it to be dark. Oh, and did you hear what she said about Dark? Dark is her dog's name, or wolf, or whatever you want to call him. He is the biggest, scariest dog I have ever seen, ever! Maybe she wants it to be dark so we can't see her, and then maybe she thinks we won't be as afraid. And I have no idea what she meant when she said she is a Guardian. I have no idea."

Lori finished and dropped backwards onto the bed. Her mind was so full of questions and worries that she didn't want to think about any of it anymore. She looked down at Sly, smiling. She was about to reach for him, but before she could he turned and looked at her. He tilted his head and then climbed onto her stomach. He found her hand lying across her chest and pushed his head under it. "He wants me to pet him. Look Jordan, isn't that sweet."

"He wants you to scratch him behind his ears. He loves that most of all." Jordan smiled. "Lori, what are we going to do? Maybe we should just forget about all this. Maybe she's not a witch, and she's not going to hurt anyone in the neighborhood. Like you said, she didn't hurt us tonight."

Lori looked up at her cousin. "Yeah, maybe. But everything about her gives me the creeps. Something isn't right, isn't normal about her, or her dog or her yard. It's like if we get even close to her place, she has power over us or something. That first night when Dark was almost on top of me, I could not move. It was as if he had me trapped. Why is it that I always feel like he's watching me? What does he want from us? I feel like he wants us to do something. That doesn't make any sense." Lori held onto Sly as she sat up in bed and shook her head back and forth.

"So, do you think she's a witch?" Jordan asked.

"Jordan, I still don't really believe in witches, but something is very odd about her. You were right about that. Maybe if I could see her....maybe then I would know, but I haven't. Oh well, who knows? Maybe it wouldn't make any difference at all.

She's probably just old looking. Hey, what was she talking about when she mentioned that car that almost hit you?"

"Oh, that. Well remember I told you about the squirrels, that day when I ran from her yard so terrified that I ran right out into the street. I didn't notice a car coming down the hill right at me. And something or someone....I don't know...somehow I got out of the way. But as I remember it, it felt like someone picked me up and moved me out of the street. I was so scared; I really can't tell you for sure what happened. I don't know how Helga could say she was the one who saved me. She was way back in her yard. She couldn't even have seen me from that far away."

"It doesn't make sense. Let's just try to get some sleep. We can talk about it tomorrow." Lori was tired, and she didn't know what to do next. Maybe everything would make more sense in the morning.

Sly had curled up by Jordan's pillow and fallen asleep. She leaned down and whispered gently in his ear. "Sly, please be good tonight. Don't make any messes!" He sleepily opened one eye and peered up at her. Jordan knew he understood her request. She layed down beside him and went to sleep.

Jordan had more dreams that night, but this time they changed just a little. They were less spooky. In her dreams, there were three little birds flying all around her. They would fly up ahead of her and wait for her to catch up with them. They kept this up until once again, she was in front of the same dark tunnel as all the dreams before.

The next morning everything got really weird. First of all, the girls woke up to loud chirping. They both sat up in bed, rubbing their eyes. Jordan looked around the room to see what was causing all the racket. She quickly discovered what it was. The little bird was back, and he brought two new friends with him. There were three tiny birds pushed up against the screen, peeking in at the girls. She jumped out of bed and ran over to the window. "Look Lori! Look whose back!" Jordan said cheerfully. It felt so good to just get out of bed and be happy, with no worries. But then, Jordan remembered her dream.

Lori was right behind her cousin. She joined her at the window, smiling just as big as Jordan was. She too felt light hearted and happy. Nothing weighed heavy on her mind this morning.

While they stood at the window, Jordan told Lori about her dreams.....about all her dreams. They both agreed it had something to do with Helga. Jordan watched the sweet little birds and smiled.

Jordan had an idea. "Why don't I raise the screen, and let them come in with us? Wouldn't that be cool?" Jordan asked without taking her eyes off the birds.

"Can you do that? The screens on my windows don't open." Grinning, Lori placed her fingers up to one of the fluffy birds and stroked his chest.

"Yeah," Jordan replied. She placed her fingers on a flat square bar at the bottom edge of the screen. "See, all you do is push this over and then....pulllll." Up it came. She moved it slowly so as not to scare them away.

Lori watched in amazement as the screen slid up and the three little birds rode with it. Their tiny heads darted about, watching every move Jordan made. She was hoping they would not fly away, and to her delight they didn't.

Once Jordan had the screen up far enough both girls moved a few steps away from the window, giving the birds some space. Jordan wanted them to come in but wasn't exactly sure what would be the best way to coax them in. She was hopeful that giving them some space would help. Now they just needed to be very still and very patient. Neither girl took their eyes off the trio. They were quickly rewarded. First one and then the second bird hopped down the screen and flew to the window sill. The third one took flight, zoomed around the bush in front of the window, and to their surprise flew right through the open window and into the room. Lori pointed at the window. Jordan had one hand held out toward Lori, as if she were ready to place it on her cousin's shoulder. When the bird flew into the room, both girls froze like statues, not wanting to frighten any of them away. They held their breath and waited to see what the brave little birds would do next.

To Lori's total amazement, the flying bit of fluff landed on her pointing finger. A sudden but delightful thrill ran through her body, starting from her finger where her new friend was perched. Her whole body felt warm and giddy. It took everything in her to hold back the giggle that so badly wanted to jump from her throat. It was as if she had been transformed from reality and placed in a fairytale story book.

Jordan's mouth flew open and a squeal struggled to escape. She dared not move to cover her mouth, but instead she slammed her lips together to stifle any sound that might escape. Her eyes nearly popped out of her head as she stared at the vision of this sweet bird sitting on her cousin's finger. Dare she try to pet it? No, she thought. She'd better not. She was very envious of this magical moment. She wanted to know what it would feel like to have a bird sit on her finger. She very slowly repositioned her hand that was already outstretched. She rotated it slightly and pointed her index finger, just like Lori was doing.

Lori was lost in this moment of joy. She had never experienced anything like this before. She wasn't aware of anything in the room except for the warm tiny toes that were gently wrapped around her finger. She watched the bird as he tilted his head and watched her. She wanted to reach up and stroke his feathers, but was afraid if she did he would fly away. Behind her, Jordan's finger was now in position, patiently waiting for her turn.

Both girls had forgotten all about Sly. He had been sleeping by Jordan's pillow, and was now awake. He climbed off the bed and sat at Jordan's feet. She nearly screamed out loud when she felt his tiny but sharp claws working at her toes. She didn't want to scream or move and frighten their visitors. What was she going to do? Sly wanted her attention. The room was suddenly filled with fluttering feathers. The two birds from the window took flight and were circling the girls. Sly started climbing up Jordan's leg. The room was in total chaos, and the girls didn't know what to do about it.

Lori turned slightly and saw Sly half-way up Jordan's leg. She didn't want her bird to be eaten, so she moved a couple steps away from her cousin's side. She didn't know what Sly might do to the little bird that she now felt responsible for. The other two birds continued to fly around the room. Lori was certain the one on her finger would join them, but to her surprise he didn't. He didn't even seem concerned. He was still looking up at her, blinking his bright round eyes and tilting his little head back and forth.

Jordan had no choice but to move. She had to pick up the frisky little raccoon before he managed to pull her pajama bottoms off her. She bent down and reached for him. He was now standing on top of her foot and he grabbed a hold of her as she reached for him. The flying duo whooshed around her head as she stood up. Sly reached out a paw as one flew by him. Jordan quickly grabbed his tiny paw and held him to her. 'Well, so much for any chances of holding a bird' she thought as she snuggled Sly close to her chest. She was sure the birds would not come near her while she was holding him, but she was wrong. She stood in the middle of the room, watching the birds fly around her. Suddenly, one of the birds came down and settled on her shoulder. The other one landed on top of Sly's head.

Lori was the first to explode with laughter. No longer could the giggles be held back. Jordan squealed as she watched Sly slowly tilt his head and raise a paw. Sly did not seem alarmed at all by the boldness of the bird. Instead he seemed almost playful about his head being used as a perch.

Jordan was thrilled to have one of the birds on her shoulder, and overjoyed that Sly was included in the fun. The silence and tension was ended. The entire room was transformed into a magical place not of this world. Only in fairy tales do people get to play with animals. It was wonderful, and mysterious. Neither girl wanted it to ever end, but it did.

"JORDAN." Jordan heard her mother calling her just outside the bedroom door. Lori and Jordan looked at each other in fear.

"Lori, what are we going to do?" Jordan whispered. She looked down at Sly and then at the three birds.

Lori didn't want the bird to move from her finger. She looked over at Jordan and shrugged her shoulders. She had no idea what to do.

"Yeah mom, we're up, we're awake. We'll be out in just a minute." Jordan hoped her reply to her mom would satisfy her. To their alarm they heard her mother take a hold of the door knob. For the next few seconds everything seemed to move in slow motion. Jordan watched helplessly as Sly jumped from her arms to the floor and then to the window sill. All three birds followed him out the window. In seconds they were all gone, and so was the magic. Sadness covered Jordan's face as the door opened and her mom poked her head in.

"Good morning girls! What do you two want for breakfast this morning?" Jordan's mom asked with a bright smile.

Fortunately Jordan had her back to the door, and her mother couldn't see the despair on her daughter's face or the silent tears that streamed down her cheeks.

Lori jumped in and saved the moment. "We want pancakes, if that's okay with you, Aunt Michelle."

"Sure, that will be fine. Everything should be ready in a few minutes." She turned to leave the room. Then she called over her shoulder, "You two come on out in the kitchen and keep me company. I haven't seen either of you for more than a few minutes at a time since Lori arrived. I'd like to visit with you both while I fix breakfast this morning."

"Sure," Lori called after her. "We'll be right there." She turned to her cousin. Jordan was looking out the window, her shoulders trembling. Lori went to her and placed her hand on

Jordan's shoulder. She knew Jordan was crushed. Sly was gone again. "It's okay Jordan. I bet he will come back. He loves you, and you know he likes being with you. The first thing he did this morning was come to you, wanting you to hold him. Everything will be okay, but you have to stop crying. You're mom will want to know what's wrong if she sees you crying."

Jordan nodded. She dragged her hands across her face to wipe away the tears, but she did not move. She kept looking out the window.

Lori continued trying to cheer her up. "Jordan, wasn't that the coolest thing, having those little birds come into the room like that? I have never seen wild birds act like that, or anything wild act like that. Have you?"

Jordan remained silent for a few minuets. Softly she replied, "Yes, once a long time ago. Remember the squirrels…the time I followed the squirrels into Helga's yard? I remember how friendly they were, and I remember thinking how odd it was for squirrels to act so friendly."

Lori let Jordan's words soak in. She thought about all the strange things that had happened since she had been at her cousin's house. "Weird isn't it?" Lori said in a low voice. "Everything seems to lead us back to Helga. Everything, even Sly." She shook her head back and forth thoughtfully. "What is going on?"

"I'm not sure, but I have a feeling we're going to find out, and we're going back to Helga's. That's where Sly went, I know it, and he wants us to come. He wants us to go back down to Helga's house."

Lori's eyes moved from the window to Jordan. Jordan had changed. She seemed more grown up. She was ready to go back to Helga's. 'But am I ready?' Lori wondered. She still didn't know what to think of Helga, and as much as she hated to admit it, she was still terrified of Dark. She had to be strong, and she wanted to know what all these things meant. She knew Jordan was right about Sly. He was leading them back to Helga's. "You know what I think? I think it's time we find out just what Helga wants from us," Lori said. "It's the only way we're going to be able to put an end to all this. Until we confront her, we will continue to make our moon light trips each night, without end. I'm sure of it."

"Yes, you're right. We have to face her, we have too." Jordan turned away from the window, took a deep breath, and walked over to her cousin. Jordan grabbed Lori's hand. We'd better get to the kitchen before my mom comes looking for us. They walked out the bedroom door and down the hall, feeling confident that they were doing the right thing.

Evening came faster than either girl had expected. They hadn't talked about going back to Helga's since that morning. They had no idea what they were going to do. They had no plan of action...nothing. That night they slipped out the back door. The first thing Lori asked her cousin was, "Don't you think we should talk about this? I mean shouldn't we have some sort of plan?"

"Lori, we have made plans every time and it hasn't done us one bit of good. Once we get near Helga's yard she has been the one in control. You even said so. I think we should be ready for anything, but mostly, let's just stay close together and be ready to run. How's that?"

"I like it. Okay, let's go." Lori responded with more enthusiasm than she really felt.

CHAPTER 11

Helga Needs Us

Once they reached the edge of Helga's yard they both stopped. Neither one of them wanted to be the first to step into the tall weeds. They were both extra cautious. They listened intently for any of the usual sounds they often heard when they were this close to Helga's yard. They heard nothing…nothing at all.

Lori searched the weeds for the pair of large eyes that were always there, but she did not feel them or see them tonight. 'That's strange,' she thought. 'What could this mean?'

Jordan reached for Lori's hand and gave it a tight squeeze. Together they stepped into the weeds. They took a few steps and then stopped. They really had no idea where the house was. It was too dark and too weedy to see it. Even though they had an idea of which direction to go, they didn't know exactly. Neither girl wanted to go stomping around all over Helga's weed patch. Then yet another mysterious thing happened. A soft glow of light fell out in front of them. It was like a path made of moon light, leading to where they were sure Helga's house was. Obediently they followed the path, and in a matter of seconds they were standing at Helga's front door. They were not about to knock. They just stood there and waited to see what would happen next. They heard a wicked scraping sound. Slowly, the front door opened for them. They did not step forward right away. Still holding hands, both girls tightened their grip on each other and slowly dragged their feet forward and through the door.

Jordan could feel her heart thumping in her throat. She was breathing heavy and she felt her legs trembling. She had to get control of herself. She had to calm down. The room was dimly lit, but she could see a flimsy looking table along one wall. It was covered with strange shaped jars and bottles, with all sorts of bright colored liquids in them. There was something boiling in a kettle over an open fire pit, and dark blue smoke rolled above the kettle and up the chimney. When Jordan saw it, she remembered when her parents had driven by late at night and she saw colored smoke coming from the chimney. How could Helga not be a witch? This is exactly what Jordan expected her house to look like. How could she calm herself down? This is not where she wanted to be. Panic was quickly taking over. This was a mistake, and they had to leave now.

Jordan pulled on Lori's hand and swirled around to run out the door. To her total and complete horror the door was gone. She took two steps and then stopped. Fear covered her face and filled her heart. How could a door disappear? There was nothing there! The wall was solid, as if no door had ever been there.

Lori was just as shocked as her cousin. Both girls stood there staring at the wall. Maybe they had gotten turned around. Maybe the door was on a different wall....maybe. Lori's eyes darted all around the room in search of an exit. Then she realized even the one small window was gone. They were trapped.

The girls wrapped their arms around each other. Jordan slammed her eyes shut. She couldn't believe this was happening; her worst fears were coming true. She swore she would never go in Helga's house, and now look at what was happening. Not only did it appear she was right about Helga being a witch, but now they were trapped inside her house. Helga had used Sly to trick them. They were probably about to be dinner. "Nooooo.... noooo!" A moan escaped her throat.

Lori held Jordan protectively close to her, but unlike Jordan, she kept her eyes wide open. She looked from one corner of the room to the other....waiting....just waiting. She knew Dark was there. She could feel him, and she was equally sure that Helga was there too. She decided to break the silence. "Why are you doing this? We trusted you. You said you would not harm us. Show yourself and let us go." Lori's voice shook even though she tried so hard to sound brave and strong.

"I spoke the truth. I will not harm you. I am so thankful that you came."

Lori's eyes moved to the direction the voice was coming from, and then she saw the bright yellow eyes. They were moving toward them, very slowly. As Lori watched the bright eyes come out of the blackness, she saw something else too. What was it? To her horror a dark raggedy figure emerged from the shadows. It was Helga, it had to be. She looked just as Jordan had described her. Her body was stooped over at an awkward angle. Her black robe-like dress was torn with many holes in it. The hood was pulled way over her head and totally hid her face from view. All Lori could see were long strands of gray tangled hair. Lori worked hard to control her overwhelming fear. So many thoughts ran through her mind. She could certainly understand now why Jordan had been so insistent that this old woman had to be a witch. Almost anyone seeing her would think that. Jordan had carried this image in her mind for years.

"Don't be frightened. Dark will not harm you," Helga said in a clear voice. *"He is here to help me....to help me tell you what I need from you. Lori, do not judge me by what you see. I am not what I appear. I will explain."*

"What do you mean?" Lori asked, feeling much braver now.

Jordan opened her eyes the minute she heard Helga's voice.

Her view was frozen on those eyes....Dark's eyes.....but then she saw Helga's stooped shaggy figure looming there near Dark. Jordan wanted to scream, but all she could do was stand ridged by her cousin's side. She silently prayed that Helga would not come any closer.

When no response came back to her, Lori asked again. "What do you mean Dark is here to help you? How can he help you? Does he protect you?"

"Yes, he protects me, as he protects both of you. He also speaks my words for me. He is my eyes, my ears, and my voice, and he is going to tell you both how you can help me. He will tell you what it is I desperately need you to do."

Lori was so confused, "What do you mean he is your eyes, ears and voice. How can a wolf talk?"

"I know all this is very hard for both of you to understand, but you will have to believe me. What I say is true, even though for most humans it is almost impossible to believe. I find that children can believe in such things much easier than grown ups can, and I have already shown you many wonderful things that are hard to believe... right?"

Lori loosened her hold on Jordan. Both girls found themselves interested in what Helga was saying. They both knew what Helga meant by the *wonderful things*. They somehow knew that all the cool things they had witnessed; the friendly birds, the squirrels and even Sly, had all been connected to Helga.

"Yes," Helga said. *"The birds, and the squirrels, and even my little frisky raccoon which Jordan has named Sly."*

Lori's eyes became large and round. Hearing Helga confirm her thoughts was a little spooky. She shivered as goose bumps popped up all over her face and traveled down her back. Taking a deep breath Lori asked, "You can read our thoughts, can't you?"

"Yes, I can. It is one of my charms or gifts as a Guardian. I have seven charms."

"What do you mean by a Guardian?" Lori asked.

"A Guardian is sort of a protector, a guardian of all. There are

only seven of us and we have been here from the beginning. We each have seven gifts or charms as we call them. They are not all the same, but they are very special. With these gifts we are able to guard and protect all things for all of eternity."

Jordan had been taking it all in, and pure joy filled her entire body as Helga spoke. Each word brought relief and comfort to Jordan, and she could no longer remain silent. The words flew from her mouth. "You aren't a witch. You are an angel!" Jordan burst out with joy. "You are an angel. That's what angels do; they guard us and protect us. Isn't that right? That's what you are!"

"Well not exactly, but I don't mind you thinking of me in that way. You are close to the truth."

"What is it you want us to do for you?" both girls asked at the same time. All feelings of fear were gone. They were relaxed, and felt almost comfortable standing in this awful, damp, dark place.

Helga responded to their question. *"I have lost something very valuable, very important. I know where it is, but I cannot reach it. But you two can. You two are very special. You are children, and you are good, kind, and pure of heart. You both have real love and tenderness toward all my wilderness friends. They are the ones who have chosen you. They have chosen you two to help me. One of my charms has been lost. Because of my carelessness in losing it, I must have you two brave children recover it for me. The charm can only be touched by humans once every hundred years. That day is only three days from now. Every detail of the retrieval must be precise. I will tell you where it is, how to get it, and the exact moment you can touch it. It will not be easy, but you two and only you two can do it. Will you help me?"* Helga's voice was pleading.

Lori and Jordan looked at each other in silence. They both knew that this was why they came here tonight. They came to find out what Helga wanted of them, and now they knew, but they both still had a lot of questions. Lori wanted to know exactly what they would have to do, but in her heart she knew she would do it, no matter what it was.

Jordan wanted to know where this missing charm was. Was it in a spooky place? Was it far from here? Helga said it would not be easy, but what did she mean by that? Would it be dangerous?

"No Jordan. It is not dangerous. I would never put either one of you in danger, but it will not be easy. If the two of you work together you can do this. You will be doing an incredible thing, something I have waited over two hundred years for. You will be helping the entire universe. You cannot imagine how important this is. I am not whole without all my charms. I am not able to serve as I was intended to, and I have lost many of my powers because of this. That is why Dark must guide you. If I can not regain the precious charm I have lost, I will eventually cease to exist."

Both girls were totally absorbed in the words Helga spoke. Her voice was soft and filled with sadness. They understood now, and they were ready to hear exactly what Helga needed them to do. They glanced at each other again. They both knew what the other was thinking, down to every detail. They looked into each others eyes and nodded. There was no need for words. They looked across the dimly light room at the shabby silhouette of Helga and smiled.

"Thank you Jordan and Lori. Thank you both. Three days from now, when darkness falls, come to me. I will explain everything else then."

Jordan was surprised that was all Helga would tell them. She had expected her to lay out the whole plan. She didn't like not knowing what they were going to do, or where they were going to go. Trying to sound brave Jordan asked, "Do you need us to bring anything with us?" She hoped this would open up some conversation and Helga would offer some details.

"No, I will have everything you need here."

"Where is the charm? Will we have to go very far to get there?" Lori asked with a little quiver in her voice. Like her cousin, she really wanted to know more. She wanted to be prepared for what was ahead of them. Lori always liked having a plan.

Helga replied, *"It is very near. It is trapped in the culvert that goes under the road in front of my house. I cannot be very far from it. If I am I will die. That is why I do not leave my yard, ever."*

Lori immediately felt guilty about her questions. She was beginning to see how Helga was suffering, and how desperate she was for their help. She was becoming very determined to do this for her, no matter how hard or scary it may be.

Jordan listened to Helga's words and felt sad. All this time she thought such awful things about Helga, how she was so ugly and weird and evil. But instead she was some sort of wonderful creature who protects the universe, and is suffering so much. Jordan began to see things quite differently. She had been so wrong about everything.

The culvert that ran under the road had always been a place Jordan had been afraid of. It was dark and dirty, and usually wet. Until now, everything about Helga's yard seemed spooky, even the culvert.

Even now, many things remained frightening. It would not be easy for her to overcome all her fears, but she felt she had to do this for Helga. She had to try to make things right for all the terrible things she had thought about her.

Silence fell over the room, and what dim light had been there now vanished. Even Dark was gone, and his eerie eyes. Lori whispered, "Helga, are you there?" Her words seemed to echo into the blackness.

The two girls could not help but reach for each other and hold on tight. They stood there in total darkness for what seemed like a long time. A loud creaking sound screeched from the other side of the room. They jumped. Their heads turned and faced the direction it had come from. Both searched the darkness to see what had caused the noise. Even though they couldn't see anything, they could not pull their attention away. Then from across the room, a soft beam of moonlight flooded in. They found themselves squinting to help their eyes adjust to the light. The door that had seemed to disappear earlier was now standing open, waiting for them to walk through it. Silently they moved together as one, through the door and out into the yard. They traveled home in silence. They were both happy, yet frightened at the same time. They both wanted to be brave, but couldn't help the heavy feeling of fear creeping in on them. And they both knew exactly what the other one was thinking and feeling.

The trip home seemed to take only seconds. Once inside Jordan's room they silently prepared for bed. No words were spoken aloud, there was no need.

The next morning came as a dark and rainy morning, but the cousin's awoke feeling more rested than they had for days. They smiled at each other and jumped out of bed, ready for the day. As they got dressed and straightened the room they heard Josh at the bedroom door. Jordan looked toward the door and said, "Come on in Josh. We're up and dressed."

Josh opened the door and stood there with a puzzled look on his face. "How did you know I was out here Jodan? I hadn't even knocked on your doow yet?"

"I heard you Josh, I knew you were there," she replied. "I am starving. Is breakfast ready?"

"Yep, mom sent me to wake you guys up," he said as he entered the room. "What aw you guys going to do today?" He looked up at them both, his big brown eyes full of hope. He had really tried to stay out of their way, but he wanted to be included in their plans today. The weather outside looked gloomy and he heard his dad talking about a big storm coming. That could mean only one thing.....no playing outside. He bounced up onto Jordan's freshly made bed and smiled. "I have a gweat idea. Since it's supposed to wain today, why don't we all pway boarwd games?"

Jordan reached for his hand and pulled him down off her bed. She looked at Lori and with a knowing smile said, "Sure, that sounds like fun. We'd love too."

All three left the room and headed for the kitchen. Both girls had a few things in mind that they wanted to do within the next three days. For Lori, the most important thing was to examine the culvert. Lori had no idea what it looked like. Would they fit inside it okay? Would they have to crawl on their hands and knees or could they walk through it? 'Stop! Stop thinking about it,' she scolded herself. It didn't really matter anyway. She knew she would do whatever she had to…..whatever she had to do. It wouldn't help worrying about it. Jordan glanced over at her with a look of understanding.

The day was filled the laughter, fun, games and snacks. The three hardly noticed the heavy rain and constant thunder. They had a wonderful day and by evening they were all worn out. Jordan and Lori didn't even let Helga enter their minds. They had played hard and they slept hard.

The next morning was a repeat of the day before. Steady rain and dark skies continued. Again, the girls didn't worry. They still had one more day. Tomorrow they would take a walk down the street. Tomorrow they would examine the culvert. But as the day moved on and the rain and clouds continued, their moods turned as gloomy as the sky. Evening was upon them and it was bed time.

Jordan went to kiss her mom and dad good night. They were sitting in front of the TV watching the evening news. Jordan heard the weatherman say, "No change in the weather for tomorrow. The rain will continue." She felt her shoulders slump. She was beginning to get very worried. She knew that when it rained, the culvert filled with water. A little rain was not a big problem, but a lot of rain…well…she remembered times when it had rained a lot, and high fast moving water rushed through the culvert. She knew that right now a lot of water was running through the culvert under the road in front of Helga's house. What were they going to do? A thought jumped into her mind. What if Helga had caused the rain? She didn't seem to want them to know much about the details. Maybe Helga knew they wanted to examine the culvert, and maybe she wanted to keep them away from it. Could Helga have caused all this rain? Surely not. If Helga wanted to harm them, she could just put a spell on them. She wouldn't have to send them on a scavenger hunt into a flooded culvert. Jordan pushed the thoughts out of her head.

Lori changed into her pajamas and climbed into bed. Her mind was also spinning with questions and concerns. Tomorrow was the third day, the day they would go back to Helga's. Tomorrow they were going to recover Helga's lost charm.

"Oh my gosh, tomorrow night!?" both girls gasped out loud.

They looked at each other. They were thinking the exact same thing. Both started talking at the same time, saying pretty much the same thing to each other. Lori slowly reached out her hand and gently pressed one finger up to Jordan's lips to silence her. The room became deathly quiet.

"What is going on Lori? Do you think Helga has control of our minds, even now?" Jordan whispered, afraid to speak her fears aloud.

"I don't know, all I know is that you and I were thinking the same thing. Do you think it's true? Do you think that Helga has caused all this rain?" Lori asked keeping her voice low just as Jordan had done.

"No, why would Helga make it rain?" Jordan responded to Lori's question. "The rain is filling the culvert, and if the culvert is full of rain we can't go in it! We would be washed away and drowned. And if we can't get in it, we cannot get the charm for her."

"You're right, Helga is not doing this. It doesn't make any sense." Lori paused and then asked, "Jordan, have you ever seen the culvert? I mean, have you explored it?"

Jordan looked at her cousin with a perplexed expression on her face. "Lori, you must remember that up until a few days ago I was sure Helga was evil. All my life I thought everything on and around her yard was spooky, and part of me still feels that way. It is very hard for me to not get a creepy feeling about most everything down there. So to answer your question, no, I have not explored it, but I have seen it."

Lori jumped up off the bed. She spun around and looked at Jordan, eager for more information. "You've seen it!? Oh tell me, tell me what it looks like. Is it big enough for us to stand in, or will we have to crawl into it? Is it really awful? Is it buggy?" Lori shot one question after another. She was so happy to know that Jordan knew what it looked like. It would be so much better for Lori if she knew what to expect. Her large blue eyes peered into Jordan's and she waited for her to respond.

Jordan thought back to her old memories. She didn't remember everything about that day; she had been very young. She was walking home from kindergarten, and a paper had blown out of her hand. It was a picture she had drawn for her mother for Mother's Day. She had been very proud of it, and eager to give it to her mom. She watched helplessly as it flew up into the air and over the edge of the road, down into the culvert. She didn't want to crawl down into the deep ditch off the road, but her pretty drawing was very important to her. The culvert was so big, and so dark. Luckily, the picture had landed on the edge of the enormous hole. She remembered seeing Dark that day. He was in the culvert. She had quickly grabbed the paper and ran home. "Lori it was a long time ago, and I was a little distracted that day. I really don't remember a lot about the culvert."

The tremendous disappointment revealed in Lori's eyes upset Jordan. She felt she had let her cousin down, so she quickly added, "But I do remember that it was very big. I bet my dad could walk through it without bending over, and my dad is taller than both of us. So I know we won't have to crawl around in there."

Lori seemed somewhat relieved, but still wanted Jordan to try to remember more. "Was it yucky? Did it look like a place where spiders would hang out?"

Jordan knew her cousin had a very real, very big fear of spiders. "I don't know, I can't say for sure......I was too busy looking at .....at.....Dark. He was there....deep in the culvert. He scared me to death. That's all I can remember.....Dark's yellow eyes shooting into mine like sharp spears." Jordan was sorry she couldn't remember more.

Lori immediately felt bad. "I'm sorry Jordan, I didn't realize. That must have been awful for you. Dark was probably guarding Helga's charm, protecting it."

"Yea, he probably was, that makes sense. A lot of things make sense now, but...but Lori, I am scared. How will we get Helga's charm if it's under water?" Jordan fell back onto her pillow.

Lori sat down on the side of the bed. She reached over and put her hand on Jordan's shoulder. She wanted to comfort her cousin, she wanted to reassure her. The problem was that Lori was having the same concerns. She shook her head back and forth and let out a heavy sigh. "I don't know, Jordan. That night we talked to Helga, I felt so good about what we were going to do for her, so brave, so sure we could do it. But now, I am worried too. All I do know is that we cannot let her down. She sounded desperate. She needs our help."

Jordan turned over and looked up at Lori. "You're right, we will go to Helga's tomorrow night, even if we have to swim to get there." A small forced smile played across Jordan's face. "Come on, let's get some sleep. Maybe tomorrow won't be as rainy. Maybe the weatherman was wrong." Jordan pulled up the covers and snuggled under them. Lori did the same. Their sleep was interrupted throughout the night by loud claps of thunder, and they both heard the hard rain drops slapping against the bedroom window. They tossed and turned all night. Broken bits of dreams filled their minds. They saw looming images of a long dark tunnel, a dark raggedy figure lying on the ground, the haunting black wolf standing over it, his head sadly hanging down. Their dreams were as one, both the same.

At last the dim morning light streamed in through the window. Both girls lay there staring up at the ceiling. They were relieved to see morning come, thankful that they did not have to close their eyes and try to sleep anymore, and happy in the knowledge that after tonight there would be no more dreams. What lay ahead of them, however, was not going to be a dream. It was going to be real, and they had no idea what to expect. For Lori, that was the worst part. For Jordan it was the best part, because if she really knew what was to come, she would be truly terrified.

After what felt like an hour of lying there in silence, Jordan heard the rest of the family moving around the house. Everyone was getting up and getting ready for a new day. Jordan wished she could get up and look forward to her day, but she couldn't. She had never felt like this before. She had never dreaded a day like she did this one. She squinted her eyes shut as the memory of her dreams flashed back into her mind. She didn't want to think about them. She kept her eyes closed tight and said a silent prayer. She prayed the dreams would go away, and never come back.

Lori's thoughts were also on the dreams that haunted her all night. She had never had such clear and vivid dreams before. She knew she had a big imagination, but still, what could the dreams mean? It had to have been Helga, lying there, with Dark looking down at her. Was Helga trying to communicate with her through her dreams? Was she trying to let Lori know just how desperate she was for their help, or had something happened to her?

Deep in their own thoughts they played out what might lay ahead of them. Lori put together a mental list of things she wanted to take with them, even though Helga said she had everything they might need. She really doubted that Helga would have a flashlight.

Jordan was thinking more in terms of water, lots of water. She was grateful that it was summer and was warm outside, despite all the rain. She loved to swim and play at the pool. She was not normally afraid of water, but this would not be clean clear pool water, and it was going to be dark, very dark. Finally she sat up in bed shaking her head back and forth. "Oh! I am so tired of thinking about this." She looked over at Lori. "Come on, let's get up and do something, play more games with Josh, or maybe mom will let us bake some chocolate chip cookies. That would be fun." Suddenly she was smiling. She jumped out of bed and shook all over, as if ridding herself of dust. She bounced across the room and pulled her clothes out of her dresser.

Lori sat up and looked at her younger cousin as if she were possessed.

From across the room Jordan looked over her shoulder and saw Lori was staring at her. "Come on," she said again, with a big smile on her face. She turned and ran toward the bed. She jumped up on it and started bouncing. She knew this was a big no, no, and if her mom saw her, she would be in trouble, but she just couldn't help herself. She had to let off some steam, and she had to stop thinking so much about tonight, about everything. "Come on," she squealed again. "Get up, let's have some fun!"

Jordan's enthusiasm was contagious. Lori felt a smile cover her face and it felt great. Jordan was right; they had to relax and try not to worry. Somehow everything would be okay….. somehow. She just had to stop thinking about the dreams….she had to. She jumped up and the two held hands and bounced around on the bed. Laughter and giggles followed. The feeling was amazing. Lori hadn't realized just how tense she had been.

They left Jordan's bedroom and ran down the hall to the kitchen. They talked her mom into letting them make cookies, and they even let Josh help. The warm sweet smell filled the house and washed away the dark gloomy day.

CHAPTER 12

Are We Brave Enough?

By dinner time both girls were subdued. They had had a wonderful day, but it had passed too quickly. Now the night faced them, and no longer could they block it out of their thoughts. Jordan found herself pushing her food back and forth on her plate. She visibly jumped when her mom spoke to her.

"Jordan, what's the matter with you? Don't you feel well? I made your favorite dinner and you are not eating. Maybe you had too many chocolate chip cookies?"

Jordan pulled herself straight up in her chair. She shot a look at Lori, then stared back down at her plate. She pasted a smile on her face and said, "Maybe you're right Mom, I just don't seem to feel too hungry, but everything tastes wonderful, really it does."

"Well, all this rain doesn't help," her mom said. "It's hard to be inside so much when it's summer-time. Tomorrow will be a better day, I'm sure."

Yes, Jordan thought, tomorrow will be a better day. That is if she survives tonight. Again her eyes locked with Lori's. They both let out a heavy sigh. The rest of dinner was filled with idle conversation, which neither Lori nor Jordan was really involved in. The girls helped clear the table and load the dishwasher. Once that was done they headed for Jordan's bedroom. It was time to prepare... prepare for whatever Helga needed them to do.

Once behind the privacy of the closed bedroom door the girls sat on the edge of Jordan's bed, neither one sure what to do next. Lori was the first to break the silence.

"Jordan, where's your backpack? Let's start getting ready." Her voice was low and flat, and didn't display any feeling at all.

Jordan slid off the bed and got down on the floor. She reached under the bed and dug around until she found it. As she pulled it out she thought back to the last time she used it, when they went down to Helga's with table scraps for Sly. A smile tugged at the corners of her mouth. "I wonder if Sly will be there tonight, I miss him." She walked over to her bedroom window and pushed the curtains aside. Evening was coming, and the sun was almost gone. Jordan raised her window and sat down on the floor, resting her arms across the window sill. As she gazed out into the coming shadows she realized the rain had stopped, and wondered when that had happened. Lori was filling the backpack with a few things she felt they should have with them. Jordan laid her chin on her hands, not really thinking about anything.

Suddenly the small bush outside her window shook and wiggled to life. Jordan heard a familiar growling sound, and there he was. Sly popped his tiny head right up from the middle of the bush. Jordan couldn't move fast enough to raise the screen and pull her little friend into her arms. This was just what she needed, just what the doctor ordered. Her squeals of glee filled the room, and in an instant Lori was at her side. This was what they both needed, a warm fuzzy friend to join them on this very important quest. Somehow they both felt better. This little guy took away many of their fears, and their worries. They both held onto him, and to each other, enjoying the wonderful lighthearted feeling that filled them up.

After lots of hugs Sly wiggled out of their arms and up onto Jordan's shoulder, then he jumped over to Lori's, causing giggles to roll out of them both. They had to cover their mouths to suppress the sound. Neither one wanted Jordan's mom to come and investigate. It was getting late and Jordan's mom would expect them to be in bed by now. Sly was full of energy. He had them laughing so hard, and their laughter only encouraged him. He ran to the bed and scurried up the side. He found his favorite stuffed toy and rolled across the bed holding it to him, as if he had missed playing with it. They watched with pure joy as the frisky raccoon played. He played for a few minutes, and then he stood up on his back legs and looked over at them. He looked over at the backpack Lori had been preparing. He went to it, at first just sniffing around it. Jordan hoped he wouldn't still be afraid of it. Then he did something that shocked them both. He grabbed the strap and pulled on it. Of course, he couldn't budge it; it was too heavy for him. Helplessly he looked over at them… as if to say, 'Let's go'.

The smiles that had covered their faces were replaced by expressions of amazement. They pulled their eyes from him and looked at each other. Yes, it was time to go. Jordan and Lori stood up and walked across the room to where Sly was standing, waiting for them. Jordan grabbed Sly and Lori picked up the backpack. It was completely dark outside now and the house was still. Everyone was in bed, and hopefully sleeping.

They had the routine down pat by now. They crept out the bedroom and quietly pulled the door shut behind them. They tiptoed down the hall, eased the back door open, and gently pulled it shut, making sure it wasn't locked. They walked down the few back steps, and out into the yard. Now they could take a breath, and now they could talk to each other. They could, but they didn't. Every step they took brought them closer to the reality of this dreaded night. The tension was seeping its way back into them. Jordan held onto Sly as tightly as she could to ease her fears. Both girls moved steadily along. There was no turning back now…no changing their minds.

There must have been clouds remaining from the storm because there was no visible moon, nothing to light their way. Lori was certain they were close if not already in Helga's yard. Remembering the flashlight, she opened the backpack and started digging for it. Just as she wrapped her fingers around it, light surrounded them. Jordan knew that her cousin was fishing for the flashlight, and sighed with relief as light flooded the weed infested yard. Lori put on her brakes and stopped. Jordan jolted into her cousin, not expecting her to stop so quickly. She nearly lost her grip on Sly. Once she had him readjusted and snuggled back into her arms she stepped out from behind Lori to ask her why she stopped. It only took a second to figure that out. It was Dark. He was there, and the light was not from the flashlight. It was coming from Dark's enormous eyes. Even with all that Helga had told them about the black beast, it was still uncomfortable to be so near him.

'Now what?' they thought. 'Where was Helga?' They stood stone still for some time and finally Lori found the courage to speak. "Helga, are you there? We are here; we are almost at your house. Helga, can you hear me?" Lori reached out for Jordan's hand and started to take a step forward, but Dark blocked their path. Lori turned slightly and tried to step around him, and again, Dark stepped into her path. He was purposely blocking them from going toward Helga's house. This time Lori stepped back a couple of steps. Again she called out to Helga, "Helga, are you there? What's going on? Dark is blocking our way to you." Lori waited, but nothing.

Jordan whispered to Lori. "Something is wrong. I have a very bad feeling. Maybe something has happened to Helga. I had an awful dream about her. Lori…..I'm scared." Jordan's whispered voice trailed off.

Lori nearly knocked Jordan over as she spun around sharply. Not even trying to keep her voice down Lori said, "You had a dream, a dream about Helga? I had a dream about her too. Why didn't you tell me?" Lori asked in amazement.

Jordan was shocked by Lori reaction. "I...I...I always have dreams about Helga. I didn't really think this one was, well...I didn't want to think about it or talk about it today." Her voice trailed off into the darkness.

"Jordan, you must tell me." Lori wanted Jordan to explain the dream to her, but her question to her cousin was sharply interrupted by a faint, weak voice.

"*Lori...Jordan...Dark will show you the way. Follow him.*"

Both girls froze; they were not real sure whose voice they just heard. Was it Helga? It didn't sound like Helga. The voice was very weak, and very hard to hear.

"*Please follow Dark. He will show you where to find my charm. He will help you with everything. Please...follow...Dark.*" The voice trailed of into a whisper.

Jordan squeezed Lori's hand. "I think that was Helga, but she sounds funny. Don't you think we should check on her? She might need our help."

Lori took a deep breath and turned to face her cousin. "Jordan, Dark is not going to allow us to do that, and if Dark won't let us, then there must be a good reason. And I'm sure it's what Helga wants. Something is wrong, but I think the best thing for us to do is what we came here to do. We must find the charm and give it to Helga, tonight...right now."

Jordan soaked up every word her cousin spoke. She knew Lori was right. It was clear Dark wanted them to do what they promised Helga they would do.

Dark dipped his head and spun around, as if he understood what the girls were saying. It was clear that he expected them to follow him, and they did. Their feet sunk into the rain soaked ground as they approached the edge of the stream of water that ran through the culvert. Jordan could feel her breathing quicken as fear gripped her by the throat. Dark's eyes illuminated the area, which only added to her doubts. The water was high, and very fast. She turned and looked at Lori. She needed to see her face, to look into her eyes, but Lori's face was shadowed. She didn't know how on earth they were going to do this. How could they get in this high water...how? Dark's eyes were shining ahead of them, facing the opening of the culvert.

"Do not be afraid," a weak voice drifted to their ears. *"Dark will protect you both. Place your hand upon his head. Follow him... trust him."*

Lori and Jordan looked at each other. Dark did not turn away from the culvert so he could not see the fear that haunted each of their faces. Reluctantly they released the grip they had on each other's hands. They moved apart, Lori to the right side and Jordan to the left side of Dark. With a shaking hand and a trembling heart Lori was the first one to move her hand slowly up to Dark's head. She held it there just above his fur for several seconds. Just standing this close to the feared creature was the bravest thing Lori had ever done. The thought of touching him was overwhelming. She shuttered, and looked over at Jordan.

Jordan knew how Dark had tormented Lori's thoughts since the first time she had seen him. Jordan had always been afraid of him too, but for her, Helga seemed far more frightening. Now they both had to overcome their deepest fears. Slowly Jordan raised her hand. She could feel her whole body trembling all the way down her legs to her toes.

Now both girls held their hands above Dark and slowly lowered them until they lay gently on top of his head. Lori and Jordan were surprised at the warmth that they immediately felt as they touched the black beast.

Dark gave them just a few seconds, and then he started moving toward the black watery hole that was just yards away from them. As they moved forward they heard a new voice speak to them. It was deep and confident.

"We will move into the ditch and then into the culvert. The charm is jammed in some twisted branches deep inside the culvert."

'Wow,' Jordan thought, 'Dark can talk too.' Her mind was

buzzing with thoughts and questions, as was Lori's. But now was not the time for questions or chatter.

"I will protect you from the current, and from the cold."

As they entered the water they felt the swift current pulling at them, then the sensation eased and after several minutes they didn't even notice it anymore. Dark kept the rushing water at bay and kept them safe. The closer they got to the entrance the deeper the water became. There were rocks and branches and all sorts of things under the water that slowed their every step. The culvert was enormous, so they wouldn't have any trouble fitting into it. The water was up to Jordan's chest by the time they actually entered the culvert. Inside, everything echoed. Even their breathing was amplified. Lori felt her own heart beating against her chest, hard and loud. She was sure the others could hear it too.

They plodded along for what seemed like a long time. They had to be close by now. Suddenly Jordan stumbled over a boulder. She lost her footing and her balance and felt herself begin to fall. To her surprise, her hand held firm to Dark's head, as if it was glued to him.

Dark immediately stopped, giving her time to get to her feet. *"You're O.K. Jordan,"* echoed the deep voice. Jordan wrapped her free hand around his neck and pulled herself up. She wanted to thank him, but didn't know just how to go about that. Slowly she tried to lift her hand, but it did not budge. They were locked to Dark. She didn't even have to dig her fingers into his thick fur.

Lori reached her other hand over to her cousin to help steady her. "Are you alright Jordan? Be careful, everything is so slippery, and the current is strong." Lori sensed Jordan's thoughts.

Jordan looked over at Lori. She had to tell her. "Lori, Dark kept me from slipping away. My hand is like stuck to him...go on...see for yourself."

"I know Jordan."

"This is the only way to keep you safe in the swift water. Jordan,

you would have been washed away seconds ago if you were not under my protection. Do not be afraid. Now let's keep moving."

They moved on through the culvert. Then something strange happened. All the sounds that had been in the culvert went silent. They could not hear the water, or splashes, or any echoes. Something was happening. Dark was changing. His entire body took on an electric glow. His long fur whisked around their fingers, strengthening his hold on them.

"It is time. The moment has come for you to retrieve the charm. The window of time is short. We must work fast. The charm is there, do you see it?"

The girls looked in the direction of the beam of light Dark was providing. It shined up above them. They saw a large twisted branch, and caught in the branch were all sorts of leaves and other branches and trash. Lori strained her eyes to search for something…anything that looked like…like Helga's charm. But what did the charm look like? "Dark, what are we looking for? What does it look like?"

"Don't you see it? It is there, just within your reach. It is there… we must hurry!"

"I don't see anything but a bunch of trash. What does it look like? How big is it?" Lori cried out.

Jordan searched the area for anything resembling a charm. They did not know what it looked like. Helga had not told them anything about what the charm was like.

"Helga, we need your help," Lori called out. "Can you tell us what it looks like?"

A small faint voice floated to them. *"Remember, the charm can only be touched by humans at a precise time only once every hundred years. The charm will show itself to you. When it does you must work fast to reach it…and you must both touch it together, at the same time. This is the only way to free it. If you don't do it together, it will not come loose, and all will be lost. Watch closely, you will see it very soon now. Don't concern yourselves with what it looks like. You will know."*

The voice faded away. They feared that would be the last time they heard from Helga. Now it was up to them and Dark.

Lori and Jordan felt like water statues. The only part of them that was moving was their eyes. They kept a close watch above them, waiting for something to happen, and then it did.

At first there was a tiny melody, it was the same sound as the music box. The sound became stronger and nearer, and as it did a tiny blue light shined like the color of the summer sky after a rain. The clearest and purest of blues shined out from the center of a clump of matted leaves. It was just above their reach. They knew they had to move fast. They stretched theirs arms as far as they could. They were close, but not close enough. They were only inches away. Dark put his front paws up on the side of the branch and the girls were able to pull themselves up high enough to reach the mass of leaves, where the charm was glowing just inside them. With their free hands they both reached into the clump at the same time, just as Helga had told them to.

"I feel it!" Jordan squealed. "Do you feel it Lori?"

"Yes, but it won't move. Can you help me wiggle it loose? It's stuck." Lori was worried that they were taking too long. How much time did they have?

Together both girls gripped the charm tightly and wiggled it upwards until they felt it slip free. The moment it was freed the girls felt warmth move from it into them. They both held the glowing blue orb tightly and slid down the branch back into the deep water. The whole culvert was lit up with yellows and blues blending together.

"Now we must hurry….hurry!" Dark pulled them around and headed out of the culvert. He bolted through the water, nearly dragging them behind him.

"Dark, slow down!" the girls pleaded.

"No. Helga is dying. We must get the charm to her quickly. We must hurry."

"Oh no, the dream was real!" Jordan cried.

Lori looked at Jordan with fear in her eyes as the memory of the dream came rushing back to her. They must have had the same dream. The girls did all they could to keep up with Dark. They got out of the culvert and then out of the water, but Dark didn't make it any easier on them. He was running fast and had not released his hold on them.

CHAPTER 13

Helga's Freedom

As they approached Helga's house Lori could see the door was open. Dark never slowed down. He bounded inside and slid to a stop. Jordan and Lori felt Dark release them and they slid to the floor. It was so dark inside the girls could not see anything at first. Within seconds their eyes adjusted enough to make out a raggedy clump on the floor just in front of them. Sadly they realized it must be Helga. Dark stood over her body, hanging his head, just like in their dreams.

"Oh no," Lori sighed. "Are we too late?"

Jordan noticed Helga's claw like hand partly hidden under her long dark sleeve. "Helga," Jordan whispered, "we are here and we have your charm for you. Wake up Helga, everything is going to be alright now. You see, here it is." Both girls were still holding the charm and together they placed the charm into Helga's lifeless hand.

Lori wanted to do something for her, but what? She turned to

Dark and asked him, "What can we do for her, how can we help her?"

Dark looked up at Lori. *"You have already helped her, don't you see?"*

She looked back to the still shapeless form lying on the floor. Lori did not see any change. She kept her eyes on Helga, watching for any signs of life, and then she noticed movement.

The dreary interior of Helga's house slowly took on a soft blue glow. Lori and Jordan both realized the glow was coming from Helga. Both girls' eyes were frozen on her as they witnessed an incredible transformation.

The glow grew brighter, and as it did, Helga's shabby form lifted off the dirty floor. As she floated there, her dark torn dress melted away into flowing clean white fabric. The long gray strands of hair that covered her face lifted up and transformed to streams of gold and silver. The glow became so intense that Jordan and Lori had to shield their eyes from the brightness. In an instant the glow softened, allowing them to lower their hands and soak in the most beautiful sight they had ever seen. In front of them floated a vision of a lovely young beauty. She was flawless in every way. She had soft delicate skin the color of sunshine, sweet pink lips and large ice blue eyes.

She gently reached her hand out toward Dark. *"Now, it is time you change back into Light my friend."* He lifted his nose toward her fingertips. A wave of bright light started at the tip of his nose and continued down his entire body, changing every strand of his fur from black to pure white. He was beautiful. His big ears perked up and his yellow eyes shined like sunshine.

Jordan's first thought was that Helga had died and that this was an angel. As if her thoughts had been spoken out loud a soft voice replied, *"No Jordan, I am not dead. It's me, Helga, but my name is not actually Helga. It's Agleh (ag-lee-uh). Jordan, I find it very interesting that the name you gave me is my true name spelled backwards. You girls returned my charm to me just in time. How I look now is how I used to look before I lost my charm."*

Jordan's jaw dropped open. "Oh my gosh, you are so beautiful!"

Lori was so happy that they had helped her. It was a very good thing they did by finding the charm and getting it to her. She knew that Helga would be able to do what she was created for; she could once again join with the other Guardians and keep the world and the universe safe for all. She felt so proud.

Helga drifted closer to the girls. *"Thank you both for your brave journey to a place where I could not go. You have saved me and helped in such a way that you will never fully understand. I am now free, and all my powers are restored. I must leave here, but we will never leave each other's thoughts. I have left a gift for each of you. It is a small thing, but I feel sure you will not only enjoy it, but find it to be helpful throughout your entire lives. Come Light, it is time for us to go."*

Jordan and Lori stared at the majestic vision in front of them. Agleh stood tall with Light by her side. She placed her hand on his head, and with that said the light once again became so bright that they were forced to squeeze their eyes shut. When they opened them, they were gone. Helga's house was empty, every bottle, every jar, all of it was gone. They were alone, just the two of them.

As they turned to leave, they heard a familiar melody. They stopped and both turned back toward the empty house. Oddly, the room was no longer empty. Their eyes followed the music to a bright spot of light on the floor. They walked over and discovered the delicate, jeweled music box. It filled the room with its calming, peaceful melody.

Many questions and thoughts jumped into their heads. They found themselves having a conversation with each other, without speaking a single word aloud. Looking at each other with an expression of realization on their faces, they knew what gift Helga had given to them. A voice came from the distance. *"This is something I feel you might need some day. Simply play the music, and I will be there for you…always."*

THE END